# 7ᵀᴴ GRADE SLEUTHS, Book 2:

# IGNACIO IN THE DARK

## By Dania Ramos

Cover design by Shawn Yaney.
Overdue Books, a division of Northampton House Press.
2019, ISBN 978-1-937997-91-5.
Library of Congress Control Number: 2018952220.

9 8 7 6 5 4 3 2

Teaching resources, author bio and information about
*The Seventh Grade Sleuths* series are available at:
www.daniaramos.com.

*For Mom and Pop*

# IGNACIO IN THE DARK

# CHAPTER ONE:
# MEETING IN TRANSIT

W e're about to take the Seventh Grade Sleuths into space.

Okay, not really. My fellow club members and I are just squished into the back of my mother's minivan having our weekly meeting. On one side of me sits Ju – we pronounce it *hoo* – Feliciano. She's my best friend. On the other side is Gunther Corrie, a former hater turned friend. He moved to our school last year.

My older brother Javier is in the driver's seat, glancing at the three of us in the rearview mirror. "I want to hear each seat belt buckle click." He drives more like a grandma than a nineteen-year-old guy.

Earlier in the year, Ju, Gunther, and I solved a strange mystery for our middle school's drama club. That's when we officially became the Seventh Grade Sleuths.

"It stinks that we've only had one real case so far." Ju whips off a yellow mitten and switches on the overhead light. She flips through the pages of her purple spiral bound casebook.

I open my casebook, too. It's got a black cover with a huge sticker of Neptune. "What about the Case of the Garden Gnome Thief?"

"Does that count? My neighbor didn't even realize he was technically stealing. Plus, he willingly returned all the gnomes to their owners." Gunther uncovers the iPad his parents gave him a couple of weeks ago. He's already an expert on NoteSketchy, an app that helps him take graphic notes by using photos and drawings that he makes with a tablet pen.

Ju shakes her head. "I vote no since we didn't need to actually investigate."

"Good point." Gunther taps on the screen to open his app. "I'll archive these notes into a separate folder, called...let's see...Non-investigation Stuff."

"Look at you guys," Javi glances up at us in the rearview mirror. "Being all organized and official, like real detectives."

"Hey, this is a private meeting," I yell. "Stop eavesdropping!"

He snorts. "What do you think this is, some kind of free Uber service?"

"Don't you need to concentrate on the road?" Ju says, super sweetly. "Our young lives are in your hands."

Javi laughs and shakes his head. "Bunch of punks. Better finish this meeting soon. I shouldn't be driving with that light on."

Since we have no current cases, we wrap up our official club business quickly. I turn off the interior light as we approach the Lenape Environmental Center's entrance, passing an electronic sign that reads: COSMIC NIGHT: PUBLIC SKY VIEWING IN THE SLOAN OBSERVATORY.

Every Friday night, they allow people to come and look through the enormous research telescope. As long as the sky's clear, of course. Down here at the base of the hill, I can't even spot the observatory's silver dome that was built to house the new telescope. All I see are the silhouettes of the trees during the dark and winding ride. Javi always puts on his high beams and drives about five miles per hour.

"Um...." Gunther's nose is practically touching the window. "Shouldn't they have street lamps on this road?"

"They keep it dark on purpose," I say. "The night sky is too bright because we're so close to New York City. They don't want to add any more light pollution because that would make it hard to see the stars and planets."

3

"Huh." Gunther wipes away the fog on the window that his breath has created.

Gunther told me yesterday he's never looked through a telescope. Not even a small one. Ju's come to the center a bunch of times with me, though. But that was back when the astronomy department only used standing telescopes they would set up in the parking lot. I can't wait for my friends to get a look at the new observatory.

We reach the main gate of the center, and Javi stops there as usual. To the right of the car, there's a small security booth with tinted windows. The glass slides open and blue light spills out. The nighttime guard, Oliver, is a skinny guy wearing a dark blue winter hat.

"Ah, my man." Oliver bumps fists – well, gloves – with my brother. I think he's a few years older than Javi. "You brought a whole party tonight."

"Whoa." Gunther whispers, staring through the window at the wall-to-wall monitors inside the security booth. "That's a lot of screens."

"Yeah." I nod. "They've got cameras all over the grounds."

A cold wind blows into the car.

"Brrr." Ju covers her face with her scarf.

Oliver turns up his coat collar against the wind. He hands my brother a parking pass. Then he shouts into the back of the minivan, "Looks like a clear night, Ig! Enjoy the stars!"

I stick my gloved thumb high in the air. "Thanks."

4

Javi drives through the raised gate and pulls into the parking lot next to the main brick building. The silver-metal-framed astronomy section hooks around with the two-story observatory dome at the far end. From this angle, I can see it in a clearing of trees.

"Whoa." Gunther's mouth hangs open. "Hey, Ig. How'd you find out about this place?"

"He's been coming here years. He's been into space forever," Ju says, like she's known me since I was born, which is pretty much true.

Gunther doesn't accept that answer. "But *something* had to get you interested, first. Like a movie or something?"

"Um...maybe. I don't remember." I slip on my gloves, avoiding his quizzical look.

For a second, Javi and I make eye contact in the rearview. He knows I don't want to answer Gunther's question with the real information. The real reason I'm so interested in the stars. "Have fun, you little punks." He winks then, as if to say, *I got you.*

There's a big huge secret I've never told anyone outside of my family. Not even Ju, my best friend in the world, knows that my father is a big shot astrophysicist. I mean, like a world-traveling-guest-star-on-cable-shows scientist dude. I almost told Ju a couple of months ago when we were given this school assignment to research our family history and our inherited traits. That innocent-sounding project turned both of our lives – Ju's and mine – upside-down.

5

For Ju, it led to her discovering a major family secret – that the father she still calls 'Papi' isn't her biological one – and that he'd adopted her as a baby. But her family never found the right moment to tell her this, before the project. Her skin and hair are really light compared to the rest of her family, and that had always made her feel like she didn't fit in. She finally ended up meeting her biological father, a Puerto Rican man with light colored hair and skin just like hers. And she found out she had a sister her age, Allie Martin, who lives in Jersey City.

So last month while Ju was learning this super-shocking truth about her family, I continued to keep the secret of my own. I chose not to include my father in my project because it would've meant revealing who he is. I wasn't quite ready for that, so...I decided to keep things private. Instead, I did the assignment about my family on my mother's side. I still feel bad about not telling Ju about my father. Maybe I will. Soon.

But not tonight. It's time for showing my friends how staring at gigantic balls of gas through a telescope can totally blow your mind.

# CHAPTER TWO:
# A NEW CASE

**F**ifteen minutes later Ju, Gunther, and I are inside the observatory, waiting our turn in line. The shutter of the dome has been cranked open so that a slice of the roof is no longer above us. Like a giant skylight, it reveals the night sky. This open space is aligned with the large end of the telescope. Since inside the observatory, under the dome, it's the same temperature as it is outside, the twenty people waiting to see the moon and Saturn are bundled in coats, hats, and gloves. There are a couple of families with young kids as well as a few adult visitors. My eyes have adjusted to the darkness. Now everyone appears in silhouette.

The computer at the desk station whirs. Kamir Fitzgerald, the observatory assistant, sits there at the keyboard. I can smell his leather jacket. I've been coming here at least once a month for a while now, so I know his "uniform." Leather jacket with black jeans torn at the knees. Two college interns – a guy and a girl – stand behind Kamir, watching his every move.

Dr. Joanne Nolan, the center's director and head astrophysicist, reminds each person about the rules of viewing through the new state-of-the-art telescope. She stomps one foot on a metal stepladder. "Make sure you don't touch the eyepiece or any other part of the equipment." Her voice echoes in the dome. "The smallest shift can greatly affect the focus."

"Hey, Soto, will we see the craters on the moon?" Gunther whispers. "Like holes in Swiss Cheese?"

Before I can open my mouth to answer, Dr. Nolan tells him, her voice clearly carrying from all the way across the room, "Sure will! We use a special filter since the moonlight can be pretty intense through the lens."

"Whoa." Gunther looks around in the darkness. "Who said that?"

Dr. Nolan laughs. "Sound travels in funky ways inside this curved roof. I happened to be in the right spot to hear you."

"Cool." Gunther grins. His teeth glow ghostly in the dim light.

Once all the little kids have had a chance to view the moon, Gunther moves up to the stepladder to look through the eyepiece. "Whoa, I can totally see the surface." He says Whoa about ten more times before stepping off the stool.

Next, Ju takes her turn. She's just as impressed as Gunther. "This telescope is way better than any I've ever looked through before."

A man, one of the guests, clears his throat. "Isn't it true that live observation through bulky equipment such as this is now...outdated?" He sounds like he's challenging Dr. Nolan.

She only chuckles. "It's true that much of the data collected can be studied at a computer. And that researchers spend less time physically in front of optical telescopes. But most people who fall in love with astronomy do so while looking through an eyepiece, not staring at data on a computer screen. Isn't that right, Ignacio?"

"Yep." I'm surprised that she asked me this question, instead of Kamir. "I mean, not that I've done real research or anything."

"What does he know?" the same rude man says, snotty-like. "He's just a kid."

"These days, kids know much more about the cosmos than I did at their age." Dr. Nolan waves me up the steps. "Go ahead, Ignacio."

I lean into the eyepiece and brightness fills the lens. Mostly white, but light gray in spots. There it is. The moon. I feel the same way I did the first time I saw it – peaceful, quiet, calm.

I hear Dr. Nolan tell Kamir, "Ignacio's the last up. Looks like the cloud cover is lifting in front of Saturn. We should target that next before it falls below the horizon."

"Sounds like a plan." Kamir glances up at the guy intern. "So, Jalani, once Ignacio's finished, what should I do next?"

"Uh...." The intern leans forward and peers over Kamir's shoulder, to get closer to the screen. "Command the telescope to move by pointing and clicking the cursor at the target object."

Kamir nods. "Excellent."

"The alignment?" asks the guy intern.

The tall, red-haired girl guesses, "Jupiter?"

The guy intern corrects her. "Nope. Saturn."

Suddenly the image is whisked away. The eyepiece jerks sideways. I jump off the stepladder, barely catching myself to avoid falling. "Hey! What's happening?"

"Everyone step away from the walls and stand clear of the telescope," orders Dr. Nolan. She rushes over behind the computer chair. "What's going on, Kamir? Moving the scope while a person is viewing isn't safe. You know that!" She isn't talking loudly, but still sounds angry.

I move away from the telescope and rejoin the other visitors.

"I...I don't understand." Kamir shakes his head, typing furiously, but the telescope continues to move at a slow but steady pace, as if it's possessed. "It's not accepting any of the commands I enter."

"Let me try." Dr. Nolan takes over at the computer, but she can't make it stop either. After a few moments she turns back to us. "Viewing time is over, everyone. Please follow Kamir in single file down the steps."

Kamir leads us down the staircase and past the reception desk into the lobby. "An exhibit on the gas giants is on display," he suggests, but he keeps pacing, frowning. His expression still says he is completely confused.

The two interns look like they want to hurl. One of the families heads for the door when their littlest kid won't stop wailing. The rest of us wander around checking out the exhibit about Jupiter, Saturn, Uranus, and my favorite planet, Neptune.

Dr. Nolan rushes into the lobby, grabbing a flier from the reception desk. "I had to order an override to shut down the computer. It's the worst possible timing!" She walks right up to Kamir and waves the flier in his face. "The festival is only a week away. We cannot be without the use of this telescope. The whole reason the research scientists are here is to work on upgrades to our equipment."

"I know." Kamir shakes his head.

In all the craziness, I'd almost forgotten the Festival of Matter is happening next Saturday. The entire center will be open with all kinds of science activities.

Dr. Nolan's face is pale, as if she saw a ghost through the telescope, instead of a star. "It's worse than that. If someone had gotten hurt, they could shut down everything. The entire center."

"The center cannot shut down," says the girl intern. "I'm two months into my internship. If I can't finish these credits, I won't be able to graduate this year. That'd be a total disaster!"

"Yeah, Julissa." The guy intern shakes his head. "Because this is all about you."

She shoots him a dirty look. "I didn't say that, Jalani."

They keep arguing, in low voices.

"Follow me," I whisper to Ju and Gunther. I lead my fellow sleuths into the empty astronomy classroom, which is decorated with models and posters of each planet.

Ju's smile is as broad as Saturn's rings. "An out of control telescope?" She looks excited about all the turmoil. Almost, but not quite, pleased.

Gunther is still peering out the door as if he doesn't want to miss the argument. Finally, he turns back to us with wide eyes. "You think it's hackers? Like international-type computer hackers? Or maybe spies?"

I tap my foot. "Why do you two seem so happy about this?"

Ju's smile fades. "It's not that we're happy something's wrong with the telescope."

I tear off my gloves, releasing my sweaty hands. "Kamir and Dr. Nolan could be out of a job if this doesn't get fixed. What if they shut it down?"

Gunther softly kicks the leg of the table nearby. "Sorry, Soto. I know you love this place."

I slide my gloves into my coat pockets. "I want to be an intern here one day."

"Even more reason why we've got to solve this case!" Ju nods. "We're talking about your future here. We're only excited because it's a mystery. And we can make a difference by solving it. That's what we do, right?"

"I'm with Feliciano." Gunther pulls open his iPad.

12

I sigh. They do have a point. "You're right. Maybe we can help."

Gunther is punching at his tablet. "Could something be disturbing the telescope from underneath? Maybe it's unbalanced at the base?"

I shake my head. "The telescope itself is attached to a solid pillar of concrete that reaches fifty feet down into bedrock." I know this because Dr. Nolan has mentioned this given data a few times during previous Cosmic Night sessions.

Ju paces past an encased display of moon rock. "It was so dark in there, it was hard to take in any visual clues."

"We'll need to know everyone who has access to the telescope." I scratch my forehead. "Aside from Cosmic Night – as far as I know it's just staff, visiting researchers, and the interns."

"Obviously. The interns!" Ju throws an arm out dramatically and it smacks into a file storage bin attached to the back of the door. A couple of pages fly out of a file like startled white birds. "Ow," she complains.

"That sounded like it hurt." I pick up the loose papers. "You okay?"

"Yeah. Guess it wasn't too bad." But she winces and rubs her hand. "What're those?"

I read the header on the top page: A24 USAGE LOGS. "Just some boring paperwork. Nothing that'll help us." I slide the sheets back into the storage file. "Did you hear that one girl intern freak out about the possibility of the center shutting down?"

"I heard someone say her name," Ju says. "Julissa."

I nod. "And the guy's Jalani."

"Hey." Gunther's eyes get wide. "Why don't we all come back next Saturday for that festival? We can do some hands-on detective work then."

"Sounds good." I nod. "So what should we call the new case?"

Ju smiles. "The Case of the Out of Control Telescope!" And just like that, the Seventh Grade Sleuths are back on the job.

# CHAPTER THREE:
# THE SOTO SIBLINGS

When we get home from the observatory, Javi slams the minivan door and rushes into the first-floor apartment of our three-family house. "Can't believe I forgot my show is on," he pants.

It's like the world might end if he doesn't catch the latest episode of *Metalworks Empire*, a reality show where these two funny guys show everyday people how to build stuff out of scrap metal pieces. Mostly furniture, but once they made a swing set that looked like a castle. Javi's big dream is to one day own a metalworks company.

I'm still in the main stairwell of the house when I hear a high-pitched yappy bark. The quick patter of four little feet flies down the steps of the second-floor staircase. Our upstairs neighbor's adorable pint-sized Yorkie sniffs at my feet. "Hiya, Cory!"

I squat to pet him, then wave up at the older woman who lives with her husband in the apartment above ours. She's short and squat, with gray hair pinned into a bun on top of her head.

"Hi, Mrs. Milcu."

She holds up the hem of her floral housecoat and carefully, slowly, takes the stairs one at a time. "Forgot to get the mail, can you believe it? Maybe today's the day I get an envelope with a big lottery check inside, eh, Ignacio?"

"Then you'll be able to spoil this little monster even more." Cory barks and jumps up, his tiny nub of a tail wiggling furiously. I scratch the top of his black and tan head. "Good boy!"

Mrs. Milcu squints at me from halfway down the stairs. "Your mother home?"

"Not yet." Ma works as a licensed practical nurse at the local hospital.

Mrs. Milcu shakes her head. "I keep telling her she's too busy. Needs to slow down."

It's true. Not only does my mother work twelve hours a day, three days a week, but she's also going to school to get certified as a registered nurse.

Mrs. Milcu smiles. "Well, you tell her I'm going to make sour meatball soup tomorrow."

"Great! We love your soup." It's delicious. Ma says Mrs. Milcu's meals are a taste of old-world Romania. Thanks to her, I know how good minced-meat rolls and sweet dough rolls with honey taste.

"Come on, Cory." She gathers her mail and slowly starts up the steps again. The hyper Yorkie rushes past like a tiny rocket, then waits for her on the second-floor landing.

We hardly ever see our other neighbors, the Tangas, a Filipino couple who live up on the third floor.

I enter our apartment, locking the door behind me, hanging my coat on one of the hooks in our narrow front hallway. Then I pop my head into the living room, where Javi and my sister, Christina, are arguing. As usual. She's seventeen, two years younger than him, but they both try to boss each other around.

"You're not even watching this!" He points to the television screen where a woman is standing on a beach, hysterically crying and kicking sand in the face of a bronzed, shirtless man. Gotta love the drama of telenovelas.

"I'm not stopping you from changing the channel." Christina is sprawled across the entire length of the sofa typing on her phone. She's wearing emoji print pajamas and furry purple slippers.

"Yeah, sure. But can't you get your lazy butt off your phone for one minute and help me find the remote?" Javi tugs his knit hat off and flings it at her. It hits the colorful painting of a Cuban street scene above the sofa before landing on my sister's lap.

Christina snatches off Javi's knitted cap and then hurls it back at him. "Nice hat hair." She smirks.

17

Javi's black curls are kind of weirdly matted against his head. But really, she shouldn't talk. Her brown hair is all stuck up in a messy pile on top of her head.

"Uh, guys?" I yank out the black rectangular remote that's sticking out from one corner of the seat cushion on the worn brown leather armchair, right next to them.

"Ha! And you were calling *me* lazy?" Christina jumps up and jabs a finger in his face. "Next time, try looking first."

"Try detaching your eyes from that phone before they grow roots into the screen!" Javi smacks her arm, sending the phone flying into the air.

"Hey," she gasps. "Watch it!"

The phone lands on the table, face up. Its screen shows a headshot of my sister smiling beneath a green header: *ASK CHRISSY*.

"What's this?" I grab the phone to look.

Christina snaps it right out of my hand. "It's my advice blog." She glares at Javi like she's waiting for his next wisecrack, but he's too busy changing the channel to notice and respond. "You know," she adds. "Like Dear Abby's advice column. Only for teens."

"Wait. But...*you're* the expert?" Whoops. That came out sounding more shocked than I meant it to. I just never would've guessed that all that time she spends staring at her phone, she's been dishing out advice online.

"Ya'll are so oblivious." She shakes her head. "I've been doing this for months. Got readers from all over the world. Brazil, Denmark, Australia. Yesterday, I gave advice to a fourteen-year-old from Vancouver."

18

Javi clicks his tongue. "If they know what's good for them, they'll do the opposite of whatever *you* tell them."

"Forget you." Christina huffs. She stomps down the hall to her bedroom, slamming the door behind her.

Now Javi is lying across on the sofa underneath the Cuban street scene painting. In it, small pastel-colored houses line a dirt road where three kids walk barefoot, each carrying a fish tied to a stick. A rooster and goat follow behind them. The thing I always found creepy about the painting is that the three kids don't have any facial features. No eyes, nose, or mouth. I used to think the artist ran out of time and just didn't get to finish it. But Ma says it was probably the painter's choice to leave them faceless, so the focus was on the neighborhood instead of the children. In any case, it kind of makes me shiver.

I head to my tiny bedroom, if you can even call it that. In my closet-sized room there's just enough space for a twin bed, a tall narrow dresser, and a chair. Javi built a metal shelf unit into the wall, so I have a place to keep my stuff for school and my favorite possession: a pair of Galactic Skyscape binoculars. Two maps are pinned up on my wall. One's a large view of the world attached to a corkboard, with a bunch of pushpins marking several cities across the world. The other is a poster of the night sky showing all eighty-eight constellations recognized by NASA. My Tía Sonia gave it to me for Christmas a couple of years ago. I've also posted articles my father's written for different magazines, like *Astroverse* and *Outer Space*, all around the maps.

19

Time to update the Sleuth notes. I flop onto the bed and flip open my casebook.

### OBSERVATION:
*The telescope appeared to be moving on its own.*

### QUESTION:
*Who or what caused the telescope to move on its own?*

### HYPOTHESIS:
*One of the college interns (Julissa or Jalani) somehow caused the telescope to move. By accident, or on purpose?*

# CHAPTER FOUR:
# GREETINGS FROM... .

O nce I'm done with the case notes, I kick off my shoes and shuffle down the hall in my socks. Halfway down, the smooth wood of the hallway turns into the linoleum of the kitchen floor. The orange tile in here is pale compared to the red-orange walls and even brighter orange cabinets. My mother told us these were the colors in the kitchen of her childhood home, in Cuba.

I immediately spot a postcard in the stack of mail on the table. Dolphins jump, following along behind a ferry. A long bridge spans the background. I turn over the card and recognize my father's slanted handwriting.

Ignacio, Javier, and Christina,

Sailing along the Moray Firth Coast, I was again reminded of our humble place in the universe. I hope someday you'll witness such views...and that I can be there too, in that moment of wonder.

Thinking of you always.
Your father,
Arturo

P.S. Ignacio, during winter solstice Inverness gets 16 hours of darkness!


Sixteen hours. That's a lot of time to observe the night sky. My father's postcards usually make me smile, even though they're a reminder he's far away in some other country, instead of with us.

Christina shuffles past the table to the fridge and gets out a big bottle of iced tea.

"Pour me some, too?" I flip the postcard over and stare at the soaring dolphins again.

"Here you go." She hands me a tall, cool glass.

"Thanks."

Christina eyes the postcard. "Let me guess. Another stunning place Pa wishes we could see because it reminds him of our humble place in the universe."

"Yeah." I take a sip of tea and prop the postcard against the candy dish. "Scotland this time."

She glares at the card. "Why couldn't he just feel his place in the universe here in New Jersey?" She scowls

22

furiously, and then whispers, "Wonder where he'll be for Thanksgiving this year."

"Yeah." I don't know what else to say.

There's so much I don't know about my father. We used to talk on the phone up until my seventh birthday. That was the day he let me down big time. The day when my brother, sister, and I all stopped talking to him. After an entire year of silence, Pa started sending us postcards from around the world. I have the whole stack on my shelf. My brother and sister never want to keep any of them.

Christina never talks about him. Whenever I ask questions or bring up our father, she almost always leaves the room. Javi usually just refers to him as if he's a cowboy. *He comes through every town but ours,* he says sometimes.

The front door to the apartment creaks open. Ma's whistle echoes down the hall. From the kitchen, we can hear her greet Javi in the living room. "Hola, mi amor."

Christina takes the postcard and slides it into the pocket of my hoodie. "Keep it. For your collection." She looks past me. "Hey, Ma. How was work?"

My mother plods into the kitchen wearing pink Hello Kitty hospital scrubs.

"Fine." She pecks Christina on the cheek, kisses the top of my head, then flops into the kitchen chair closest to the hallway. "Ay, it feels good to be off my feet. How was your visit to the environmental center, Ignacio?"

"The telescope went out of control! It was nuts." I throw both hands in the air. "Moving around on its own, like it was possessed or something."

Ma raises her eyebrows. "Possessed?"

Christina laughs, leaning against the wall. "A demonic telescope. That's a new one. Let me guess. Your little club is all about this mystery."

I nod. "It could be caused by something technical, but it might be human error, too."

Ma sighs and nods. "Humans make a lot of errors."

Javi saunters into the kitchen. "Except for Christina. She's perfect."

My sister crosses her arms. "When did I ever say that?"

He points at her. "You know she's got an advice blog?"

"Of course." Ma leans back in the wooden chair. "I'm a subscriber."

"No way." Javi grabs a Dr. Pepper from the fridge and pops the tab.

I laugh. "For real, Ma?" It's funny to think of her getting email updates from my sister.

Christina smiles. "She even comments sometimes."

"It's a great site." Ma covers her mouth and yawns. "Helpful content. Looks pretty."

"More than I can say for your face." Javi holds out an arm and jabs an index finger right at Christina's nose. "Ha ha!"

"Javier." Ma lifts her head and shoots him the evil eye.

My brother quickly drops his arm. "Fine, fine. I'm sure your fancy website is the prettiest of them all, Ms. Know-It-All." He does a mocking curtsy and leaves the kitchen.

24

Ma shakes her head. "Ese niño and his sick sense of humor."

When Christina sits next to her at the table, she taps her glass with one pink-painted nail, suddenly all serious. "I could take my site to the next level. If I had my own computer."

Here it comes. Christina's never-ending plea for better electronics. I'm surprised she has the guts to bring it up now, though, when our mother's clearly so exhausted. Unless...maybe it's the perfect strategy. Will she be too tired this time to say no?

Ma pats the short curls on her head. "I can't afford to buy you a computer, Christina. But I can see about contacting your father and asking him for-"

Yikes. This is always where things can turn ugly.

"No. Forget it." My sister scowls and shoves her chair back.

"Well, then." Ma shrugs. "You'll make do, using your phone and my laptop."

Christina stomps across the kitchen and tosses the empty tea bottle into the recycling bin under the sink, then slams the cabinet door shut so hard everything rattles. She stomps on, out of the kitchen. This is the kind of response I'm used to from my sister.

It's like she doesn't want to need my father at all. But she can't deny that he does help. Child support, Ma's tuition for nursing school, cash on our birthdays. Around Christmas, he sends a gift-wrapped present for each of us, but Christina refuses to accept any of them. Instead, she donates hers to the library's holiday gift drive.

My mother and I sit in silence for a moment. I take out the postcard and slide it toward her. "He's in Scotland now."

She smiles, her face kind of sad. "Looks beautiful there."

Does she wish she could have been there with him? I can't tell. "Ma?"

"Si, m'ijo."

"Would it be okay if I asked Pa for a gift?"

She sighs. "You're not getting a cell phone until you're in high school, even if your father wants to buy it for you. Javier and Christina had to wait and so will you."

"All right." I don't bother telling her that I gave up on the whole phone thing months ago. What I really want is a telescope. I mean, yeah, I've got this really cool pair of binoculars I use to view the stars up on our flat roof. But lately, I really wish I had my own standing telescope to set up instead. "Can I, um. Borrow your laptop?"

She narrows her eyes at me. "Is this for school work? I don't want you up too late."

I peek down the hall. The door to my sister's room is closed. "I just...kind of wanted to see Christina's blog."

"Aw." She tilts her head and presses both hands against her chest, over her heart. "That's so sweet."

"Come on, Ma," I say. "It's not a big thing, okay?

She holds up one hand while reaching into her tote bag with the other. "I know. But I'm your mother, and I'm allowed to think it's sweet that you want to read your big sister's blog." She hands me her laptop, along with a goofy smile. "Ten minutes. Leave it on the table when you're done."

"Thanks."

She kisses the top of my head, and then pads down the dark hall to her bedroom.

I open the computer and search for: *Ask Chrissy and teen advice blog.*

Her site appears on the first page, five listings down:

### Ask Chrissy: Anonymous Advice for Teens from a Teen

I click on the link, and it takes me to the same green page I saw on her phone, earlier. On the sidebar, it says she's published over two hundred posts, and there's a list of tags you can search by. A pink SUBSCRIBE NOW button on the same side that shows she's got over two thousand followers. Wow. That's impressive.

Before I can read further, Christina opens her bedroom door. She clomps down the hall toward the kitchen in her fuzzy slippers. "There's my phone." She yawns and crosses the room to grab her cell, which is lying next to the dish rack. She rubs her eyes. "Kind of late for homework, isn't it?"

I quickly close the browser, so she can't see that I'm on her blog. She's already got a big enough head as it is. I shut the laptop and slide it to the center of the table. "Yep. All done."

I stand quickly and make my way to my own room and flick on the light. I set the postcard of the Moray Firth with all the others stacked on my shelf. Then I grab a pushpin and kneel on my mattress to get closer to the world map on my wall. I zone in on Scotland and stick a pin at the northern end, just above the pin for Edinburgh. I wonder if my father is still in Inverness. Or if by now he's already moved on to the next place.

# THROWBACK: FOURTH GRADE PIN DOWN

This all started the Sunday before the last week of fourth grade.

Father's Day, to be exact.

That entire day, I'd carried Pa's most recent postcard in my pocket. It was a shot of cliffs on the Canary Islands, a place off the coast of northwestern Africa.

That day Ma took me, Javi, and Christina out for lunch. On the way home, we stopped at an office supply store. While Ma got stuff for her nursing school course, I roamed the aisles. Passing boxes of ink and toner, super-fancy office chairs, and a display of a large colorful board map of the world. I pulled a still-wrapped foam board map from the rack beneath it, snapped up a box of colored pushpins, and then joined my family in the checkout line.

When I got home, Javi hung the foam board map on the wall next to my bed. I found New Jersey, estimated where Dolton would be, and stuck in the first pin to represent our house. Then I slid my father's latest postcard from my

29

pocket. The Canary Islands, which were only a couple of dots on the other side of the Atlantic Ocean.

I went to my shelf and pulled out the stack of dozens of postcards he had sent us. I spread them out on my bed. One by one, I stuck a pin into each city represented in the stack of cards: Salta, Argentina. Coonabarabran, Australia. Mauna Kea, Hawaii. South Pole, Antarctica.

Every time a pin broke through the paper and sank firmly into the foam board underneath, the closer my father seemed to be. The less I felt his absence.

# CHAPTER FIVE:
# CONTEST ANNOUNCEMENTS

On Monday, Gunther saunters into homeroom a few moments before the bell sounds. He drops his backpack under the desk and slides into the empty chair in front of me.

"Whoa! Just in *time!*" Elijah Roberts whispers one seat over from me.

Elijah was a key witness in the Case of the Backstage Vandal. He always sounds like he's super excited about, well, pretty much everything.

He pokes my arm. "Remember what's *happening* today? We get our nomination forms to choose our next *field trip.*"

The bell rings. Mr. Orin stands up, smoothes his tie, and then marks attendance. A single yawn from one desk spreads, traveling from kid to kid, contagious as a head cold. It skips only over Ayesha Malloy, who is too busy checking out her hair by using her camera phone to notice anything about the rest of the world.

"I know that's not a cell phone I see, Ms. Malloy," Mr. Orin says, without even looking at her.

Ayesha quickly slides it back into her purse. Her neat black braids look as perfect as ever. Last year, when we all started here at Dolton Middle School, some of the girls began obsessing about things like hair and clothes and makeup. One them was Ayesha's friend, Sara Baker, who hasn't talked to us much once we solved the mystery of how her name ended up all over the scenery from the drama club production. Thank goodness Sara isn't in homeroom with us. I've never trusted her. Not for a second.

The morning announcements start. Franklin Diaz's voice blasts through the intercom. *"...the debate club meeting is after school...the sixth grade is collecting cans for the local soup kitchen...there's pizza and Salisbury steak for lunch today...."*

And then comes the big announcement Elijah's so excited about.

*"All students in the seventh grade will participate in the Choose Your Own Field Trip Contest,"* Franklin reports over the intercom. *"Any student who wants to nominate a location for the spring field trip can submit a form explaining why it's a good choice for an off-campus educational experience. Please hand in all entries to your homeroom teacher no later than one week from today."*

"Whoa. It's like a real *democracy* today," Elijah whispers. "That's *super* cool."

When the announcements are over, Mr. Orin passes out the Choose Your Field Trip forms. "I pushed for the nominations to happen online." He shrugs and sighs. "But yet again this year, it looks like we're sticking with paper."

Mr. Orin is really into using online tools whenever he can. He says it's his duty as a biology teacher to make his classroom have the lowest carbon footprint possible. One of his main goals is conserving trees, so he tries not to waste a single sheet of paper.

I tuck my nomination form into the front pocket of my backpack. When the bell rings, we don't have to switch classrooms since our homeroom is the same as for our first class of the day. Science. My favorite, of course.

By the time I walk into the cafeteria at noon, I've pretty much forgotten about the Choose Your Field Trip form. I toss my backpack underneath the bench and slide into my usual spot at the end of a long, white foldout table, across from Ju. Then I set my lunch tray down – pizza, fruit punch juice, a big chocolate chip cookie.

Gunther flops on the bench beside me with his tray, which holds a matching lunch. "What's the word?"

"Hey." I chomp down on a slice of pizza.

Gunther opens the cover to his iPad. "So, I was looking at some pictures I took with my iPad while we were inside the observatory on Friday night."

Ju yanks open a bag of popcorn. "What'd you expect to happen without a flash? It was pitch black in there."

"Some moonlight was coming in, though." Gunther scrolls through the camera feed on his tablet. "Thought maybe I'd get a decent image of the computer screen. Check it out."

At first glance, the iPad screen looks entirely black. Then I spot a small red dot in the corner. Which is strange. "I've never seen that red light before. And I've been in the observatory a lot of times."

Ju shrugs. "Maybe it's just never been lit while you were in there."

"Maybe," I say. "You're sure it's only in one photo?"

Gunther nods. "What do you think it could be?"

I stare hard at the little red light. "Um...anything, really."

Ju stares at the picture again. "We'll have to check it out when we're back at the scene of the crime."

"We're not sure it's a crime though," I remind her. "Someone could've done something to cause it, unintentionally. Or it could be something actually wrong with the telescope itself."

"You're right." She taps her pen against the lined paper. "Best to keep an open mind early on. Not exclude any cold hard facts too soon."

I gulp down fruit punch. "I've got more details on the scope." I pull out my casebook and show them the notes I took about the Andromeda 24" series.

"Oh, good." Ju sighs with relief. "I started researching them. And there's sooo much info. Kind of overwhelming."

"Nice work, Soto. You know your stuff." Gunther takes a big bite of his chocolate chip cookie.

"Question is...." Ju drums her fingers on the table. "How does the little red light in Gunther's photo relate to the telescope?"

"Right. That's something else we have to solve." I take out a pen and add our latest notes to the case file.

## RESEARCH:
*Classical Cassegrain reflector telescope.*
*Andromeda 24" Series.*
*20-foot dome. Concrete base.*


## OBSERVATION:
*There's a strange red light that appears in a single photo taken inside the observatory on the night of the incident.*


Today, like most weekdays, Ju and I meet up at the edge of the baseball field to walk home after school. A cold wind is blowing hard as we start off. I shiver and tug the zipper on my coat as high as it'll go. We pass along a couple of residential streets before turning onto West Avenue, which is lined with old brick storefronts. Ju slows down when we reach the gazebo the town uses for events like concerts. We step up onto the gazebo.

Someone's already inside there, lying on one of the benches.

"Hey, uh..." A guy about, my sister's age sits up. He's wearing a green army coat and has a long blond ponytail that hangs out of a gray wool hat. He throws his legs off the bench and his black sneakers land square on a skateboard on the floor of the gazebo. "Sorry," he mumbles. "Just looking for a quiet place."

I wave a hand at him. "No problem. You can stay. We'll find somewhere else to go."

"Nah, man." The guy stands on the skateboard. "I'm good." He takes off, whizzing past us, flying down the steps as if they are really a ramp, and then speeds off down the walkway.

"Think I saw that same guy skating in front of the library the other day." Ju's curly blond hair poofs out past her earmuffs.

"Bet he goes to school with my sister." I sit on the bench, the wood is cold against my legs. "Oh, hey. Speaking of Christina. I found out she's this big online guru. She's got an advice blog for teens."

"Cool." Ju pulls out her cell phone from her messenger bag. "I can try to look it up on my phone. My parent's put restrictions in it, though, so I can't promise I'll be able to get through."

"It's AskChrissy.com."

She yanks off her yellow mittens and types into the phone. "I'm in. Wow. She's got a lot of subscribers." She taps the screen. "There. Now I'm one, too."

"Wait. What?" I lean over her shoulder to see the screen, which reads: You are now subscribed to Ask Chrissy! "Hmm. Didn't think you'd be interested in following my sister's blog."

"Aren't you?" Ju scrolls through the post feed.

I shrug. "Christina already thinks she's all that. She'll get too big-headed."

"Oh, Ig." Ju minimizes the screen and slides the phone back into her coat pocket. "Your sister's head won't explode if you subscribe to her blog. Honestly, if I'd known about this last month, I probably would have asked for her advice on the whole family drama."

"Seriously? Like before coming to me?" I kick a pebble across the slats of the gazebo.

"Don't know about that. I mean, maybe just during those couple of weeks when..." she says, quietly. "You know."

I stand and walk over to where the pebble landed. "Yeah. When we weren't talking." Things got so intense back then, with the whole genetics project, we kind of forgot to be best friends for a little while.

"Yeah." She smiles. "But then I did come to you. Because you are my best friend. The only one I could trust with my big family secret. And I'm glad you were the one who was there for me."

"Me too." I nod. "I'm happy everything turned out okay."

"Yeah, I know we're good." She laughs a little and jumps up. "I'm so glad we're done with big secrets. Aren't you?"

Suddenly, I'm not cold anymore. I'm sweating underneath my puffy down coat.

"Yep. Sure am." I want so bad to blurt out, *If it makes you feel any better to know this, I've got a big secret too.* But how do I tell my best friend, *Oh, by the way, my invisible father? He's a superstar scientist – I just never told you about him.*

"What's wrong?" she asks, frowning a little.

I shake my head. "Nothing."

We walk farther down the road until we reach the intersection in front of Frank's Pizzeria. This is where we always split up, to go our separate ways home.

"See you tomorrow." Ju waves with a yellow mitten, and then starts off down the street.

As I walk toward the south section of town, the streets get narrower. The houses with big yards and three-car garages turn gradually into tall, narrow multi-family homes. Mixed in are a couple of blocky apartment buildings, and a bunch of little restaurants – Indian, Peruvian, Turkish.

My neighbor yells to me from his porch. "Ignacio, the Starman!"

"Hi, Mr. Jones." I wave back as I pass by.

Maybe the best part about living in my neighborhood is that almost all the buildings have a flat roof, including ours. All I have to do is climb the back stairwell that leads to the top of our building. From there I can look up at the stars any time I want.

# CHAPTER SIX:
# THE ROOF

L ater in the evening, I'm in the kitchen with Ma, Javi, and Christina. The air is thick with the scent of savory beef stew. Christina and I are eating big bowls of it at the kitchen table. Javi stands at the counter, sucking his down like his mouth is a wet vac.

"Come on, Ma," he says between slurps. "Play hooky just this once."

"Skipping class won't help me get this degree any faster." She shoves textbooks and notebooks that are piled on the kitchen table into her tote bag.

Javi sets down his bowl and wraps his arms around Ma. He leans his head on her shoulder. "You're such a goody two shoes."

She huffs, hooks the tote bag on one arm, and grabs her laptop bag with the other. Then she kisses each of us on the forehead. I get a whiff of sweet, fragrant honeysuckle body spray. She totters away down the hall under her studious load. "See you kids later," she calls, before the front door clicks shut behind her.

Christina sits across from me with a bowl in front of her, staring at her phone as she eats. I chow down on my stew while reading the latest issue of *Astroverse* magazine, which came in the mail today. I flip to a feature article about Dr. Lin Cho. She's the author of this amazing book, *Collision Course.* Ma brought me a copy last summer, and I read it in a week. In the book, Dr. Cho talks about the odds of our planet being destroyed by an event like Shoemaker-Levy 9. That was when this crazy series of comets collided with Jupiter back in 1993. In the magazine interview, Dr. Lin Cho mentions that she's going on a book tour. I stare long and hard at the words: **Festival of Matter, Lenape Environmental Center, South Woodhurst, New Jersey. November 13.**

"Hey, I can meet Dr. Lin Cho! Wow, wow, wow."

Christina snorts. "You care more about what's happening in outer space than down here in the real world."

Javi rolls his eyes. "So the kid's into the stars. What's the big deal?"

I stand so fast my chair nearly falls backward. "I'm not a little kid." I can't stand it when they talk about me like I'm not there. Like I'm still in pre-school.

He flaps a hand at me. "Relax. I'm defending you, bro."

40

"Anyway, you should hardly talk." I glare at Christina next. "You care more about *cyberspace* than the real world down here."

"Nice comeback." She laughs out loud. "Hey, I saw that Ju subscribed to my blog."

Javi downs a swig of iced tea. "That's so cute. You've been talking to your friends about Christina's blog."

"Thanks for spreading the word." Christina holds the phone close to her chest and bows her head regally, like she's accepting a Pulitzer Prize or something.

I stab a chunk of potato, avoiding her gaze. I just can't take my sister and her fake sweetness right now. "Ju must've found it by herself. I didn't say anything about it. I've never even seen your blog, except once for a second on your phone the other day."

She narrows her eyes. "Huh. You sure about that?"

"Yes." Gritting my teeth, I fold my magazine under one arm, rinse off my plate, and head to my room for some peace and quiet.

Back in the kitchen, about twenty minutes later, Christina's still at the table. I pass her quickly, looping my binoculars strap over my neck, ready to head off to the back stairwell.

"I know you visited my website." She clears her throat. "Even if you didn't subscribe."

I stop in my tracks and turn to look at her. "What, like, from website stats or something?"

She shakes her head. "I used mom's computer after you went to sleep on Friday. You didn't close out the Internet. You just minimized it."

I really want this conversation to be done so I can get up on the roof and look at the sky. "Fine. Yes. I visited your blog, okay? Looks nice. I wouldn't go with that shade of green for the background, though."

"Let me guess." She folds her arms and leans back in the chair. "You recommend stars, planets, maybe a few rocket ships."

I roll my eyes. "I don't care what you do with your blog, okay?" I escape at last through the door that leads to the back stairwell, where the walls are lined with faded brown panels. The linoleum on the steps is curling up at the edges, the surface worn in spots. Cory, the Milcus's Yorkie, wildly barks inside their back door as I run the three floors up to the roof. For such a small dog, he sure can make a big racket.

Even in my coat, hat, and gloves, I immediately shiver when I step out into the early November chill. Wood smoke from a few nearby brick chimneys clouds fills the air. It smells like a fall bonfire out here.

A few feet away, someone coughs and sniffles. A hooded figure, sitting with his arms wrapped tight around his knees, staring off into the distance.

It's Javi.

"What're you doing up here?" I didn't plan on having company. I was looking forward to being alone.

He gets up, not even glancing at me. "Roof doesn't belong to you."

"Never said it did." I walk toward him.

"Just...um, clearing my head," he mutters and sniffs again. "Can't let Ms. Bossy downstairs get to you, you know. She just doesn't want to be reminded of him."

"So what else is new?" I shorten the strap of the binoculars.

He exhales hard. "Funny, right? If only Christina had some advice for three siblings who don't talk to their celebrity scientist father."

"Javi." I clear my throat. "Do your friends even know who Pa is?"

My brother folds his arms and leans them on the brick barrier. "Only a couple." He takes a deep breath. "Look, Ig. I don't waste a lot of time talking about him. Why should I?"

"You think it's weird I've never told Ju?"

He looks surprised. "Really? I thought you two told each other everything."

I shrug. "Yeah, but not this. I feel like a bad friend because I haven't told her."

"Nah." He chuckles. "I don't believe she'd ever think that of you."

But Javi doesn't know about the drama that went down a couple months ago. How we didn't talk for a couple of weeks because of...well, because of me. I was the one who stopped talking to Ju when she started obsessing over Sara's theater case, and then her own family mystery.

"Hey, come on." Javi playfully punches my arm. "Ju's lucky to have a friend like you. Besides, you don't really know Pa. None of us do. So there's not much to tell." He stares east, toward the New York City skyline in the distance. "You don't remember living with him at all, do you?"

The cold breeze blows harder. I shiver again. "N-no."

"Well, you were just a baby." He shakes his head. "Christina took it real hard. She couldn't understand why Pa was gone all of a sudden. And then he starts popping up on television like some kind of rock star? Wasn't easy for her to see that." He shuffles over to a plastic patio chair and sits. "I know what Ma's told us all these years. How keeping his job meant traveling all the time. That he wanted to fly us all around the world. But Ma...she wanted us to have a stable, normal life."

"Yeah. She told me the same thing." Honestly, I know how lucky we are that Ma's putting us first. And how hard she works.

He sighs. "She wants what's best for us. Good schools. A real home. Not moving every few months."

"Right." I uncap the lenses of my trusty Galactic Skyscape binoculars and stare up at millions of stars within the Perseus constellation, wondering what our lives would've been like if we'd traveled and seen the world with Pa.

# THROWBACK: THIRD GRADE
# REFLECTED LIGHT

I still remember how heavy the Galactic Skyscape binoculars felt in my hands back when I was eight. I'd talked so much about the stars and planets, my mother bought me the pair as a Christmas present.

It happened to be a full moon that night. I made my way up the back staircase, one gloved hand checking my pocket for the postcard my father had sent for Christmas. Atacama Desert, Chile. Home to three astronomical observatories. I imagined it was a warm night and I was heading up the steps of an observatory in the Chilean desert, where my father was waiting for me.

But really I was on our roof in Dolton. I held the binoculars close against my scarf as I pushed against the heavy metal door that had been left open a crack.

Javi was already up there, waiting for me. "What took you so long, little bro?"

"Ma was attaching the strap. She's afraid I'm gonna drop them."

"Well?" Javi bounded over to stand next to me. I could practically feel excitement bouncing off him. "You gonna look at the sky now, or what?"

I lifted the double eyepiece to my face, trying to hold the binoculars as still as possible. I slowly tilted them up, turning my gaze to the clear night sky. There she was, the moon. Shining a piercing white, so bright it took a moment to get used to.

"So?" He lightly tapped my foot with his. "Is it full of cheese, or what?"

I laughed and held out my binoculars to him. "Take a look for yourself."

No, I wasn't in the Chilean desert with my father. But I remember my brother with me up on the roof that Christmas Eve, peering up at the moon and beaming his own kind of light.

# CHAPTER SEVEN:
# FESTIVAL OF MATTER

It's Saturday night, and Gunther and I stand in the lobby of the packed astronomy section at the Lenape Environmental Center, waiting for the observatory to open its doors to the Festival of Matter visitors. Earlier, we walked the Jersey Devil trail. It was kind of chilly, so we only went as far as the little amphitheater. Built out of local rock, it stands there in the middle of the woods.

Ju should be here soon. She's coming straight from her sister Allie's gymnastics meet.

I glance at the cover of the program for the Festival of Matter. There's a headshot of Dr. Lin Cho holding up her book, *Collision Course*. My own copy of the book is in my backpack. I brought it along so she could sign it.

I flip to the back of the program. "Hey, Gunther. check out these field trips."

## LEC Field Trips!

The Lenape Environmental Center offers unique educational opportunities for schools and community groups. Learn about the natural world!

### Explore the Barton BioSphere
All ages can discover the diverse array of flora and fauna found in New Jersey and the greater New York City metro area.

### Walk the Jersey Devil Trail
Our trail system features spectacular views of the New York City skyline and includes paths for all levels, including the fully accessible Devil's Horn Loop.

### Spot the Stars in the Sloan Observatory (requires night visit).
Bring the stars and planets into closer view with our research-grade classical Cassegrain reflector telescope (Andromeda Series).

### Science Slumber Party (overnight stay required, breakfast provided).
Stay overnight and experience all the Lenape Environmental Center has to offer, including the Barton Biosphere, the Jersey Devil Trail, and the Sloan Observatory.

"Ig! Gunther!" Ju runs up behind us, and motions that we should huddle close together. "Boy, do I have updates! I saw Oliver, the security guard, on my way in. Asked him some questions about security cameras. You know, pretending I was really interested in how security works here. He never guessed I was actually grilling him for info on the case."

"So?" I lightly tug at her light blue coat sleeve. "What'd you find out?"

She glances around the crowded lobby as if checking for possible spies, and then leans back in. "They have infrared cameras set up inside the observatory so they can see what's going on in the dark. All the videos from last week were reviewed, and Oliver confirmed that none of the interns touched the computer last Friday."

Gunther frowns. "So you're saying the interns are innocent?"

I scratch my head. "There goes our first hypothesis."

"Yep. Time for a new theory." Ju exhales, her amber eyes shifting to look right at both of us. "So it seems like we probably won't find an answer tonight. Oliver told me they're not letting the public view through the telescope tonight."

"What?" I frown. That was what I was looking forward to the most. "Are you sure?"

"Too risky with this huge crowd, since they still don't know what caused the malfunction." Ju shrugs. "We can walk through the dome, but that's it."

"Ah, man." I shake my head.

"At least we'll get some *investigative* observation in," Gunther says just as Kamir pulls the doors to the dome open. The line starts to shuffle forward.

I sigh, still disappointed. "Yeah. I guess."

About an hour later all four of us are sitting in the auditorium, waiting for Dr. Lin Cho's presentation. I'm seated farthest into the row, then Gunther, then Ju, who's on the aisle.

"Ugh." I lean back in the seat. "I was hoping to see Venus. Or at least spot another clue for our case."

"We were herded through so quickly." Ju shakes her head. "So now what?"

"Not so fast," Gunther whispers. "I spotted the source of the red light even though it wasn't blinking just then. The tiny bulb was right alongside the computer."

Ju smacks his arm. "Why didn't you tell us before?"

"Well, I couldn't say anything inside the observatory. Not with those weird acoustics? No way. Kamir might've heard us and figured out what we're up to."

"Look, there's a label above the bulb." Gunther flips his iPad around. "See?" The image on its screen is dark, but there are bold black words above the unlit bulb. A little sign that reads:

ACCESS

Ju scratches her head. "Huh. Maybe the red light just blinks to let you know someone's been granted access to the computer?"

I bite my lip. "Maybe we're getting too stuck on this red light for no reason. What we need are some new suspects."

A hush falls across the auditorium as Dr. Nolan comes on stage and stands at a microphone. "Ladies and gentlemen, the Lenape Environmental Center is thrilled to welcome cosmologist and author Dr. Lin Cho as our guest speaker for the Festival of Matter."

Electronic music floods the auditorium. Dr. Cho bounds up the steps to lots of applause. Her straight, shiny chin-length black hair bounces as she strolls across the stage in tall high heels.

"It's like she's a rock star or something," Gunther whispers.

Dr. Cho takes the microphone. "Hello, everyone. Before I start talking, let's spend a few moments taking in some of the exquisite photos included in my book." She turns around just as the lights dim and the large screen on the back of the stage illuminates with images of galactic collisions, stellar explosions, and asteroids crashing into planets. The digital slide show ends with the picture on the cover of her book. Orange and white swirls dotting Jupiter that make it seem like the planet's been attacked by ginormous bullets in a planetary shoot-out. It was taken back when the fragments of Comet Shoemaker-Levy 9 slammed into the surface of the planet.

After the slideshow, Dr. Cho reads from her book. Then she takes a bunch of questions. Once the presentation is over Dr. Nolan returns to the stage. "Dr. Cho will now be available to sign books in the main lobby."

I'm so glad I tucked my copy into my backpack.

We wait and let the lecture hall mostly clear out, before finally heading up the aisle.

"Guess we'll have to come back next weekend to investigate some more," Ju says, looking disappointed.

"Ignacio," a deep voice says from behind me. There's a hint of a Cuban accent in it. I turn and stare in shock. There's a man wearing a dark gray suit jacket on top of a lilac button-down shirt, blue jeans, and running shoes. He's looking at me.

My father. It really is him. There he stands, eyes glistening. "I was hoping you'd be here tonight," he says.

My throat tightens so much it hurts. For a second I feel sure I must be dreaming.

A little kid speeds past us gripping a chunk of soft pretzel in one hand. The air is suddenly heavy with the scent of salt and warm dough. I feel a wave of nausea. This is no dream. My father is here, all right, totally flesh and blood.

"Hi," I whisper. It feels like I'm surrounded. The fabric of my friends' coats rustles only inches away. Everything sounds muffled, like we're underwater. That's how my arms and legs feel, too. Heavy. Hard to move. It's as if sound and gravity have been altered for me, forever.

# THROWBACK: FIRST GRADE
## SMELLING SALT

For my seventh birthday, Ma took Javi, Christina, and me to the New York Museum of Natural History. We spent the morning doing the dino and whale tours, then waited in the museum's main entrance for my father to show up. He said he would be there. That he was coming for my birthday, straight off a flight from Europe.

So we waited. And waited.

At last, Ma checked her phone, looking worried. "He definitely said to meet him by the Barosaurus."

The visit was supposed to have been a dream come true. Pa was scheduled to be interviewed on a television show in New York City the next day. He was arriving a whole day early so we could celebrate my birthday in person. He'd gotten us free VIP tickets to a show at the famous Hayden Planetarium. I was very excited about seeing the show, of course. But, to me, the best gift would be seeing my father. That had last happened five years before, when I was two. And so I had no memory of it. It felt as if we were about to meet for the first time. All he had to do was show up.

I chomped on a huge, warm soft pretzel, thick with the smell of buttery dough and coarse, crunchy salt.

"Slow down." Christina tapped my shoulder in warning. "Scarf that whole thing down too quick, and you'll make yourself sick." She was all of twelve at the time.

"Hey, Chris," Javi, who was fourteen back then, asked. "You ever think it'd take this long to see him again?"

"We haven't seen him in, like, five years." She kept her gaze glued to the dinosaur bones. Her fists were clenched at her sides. "He's not showing up, is he?"

Ma glared at the main entrance. As if, could she only stare hard enough, then he'd appear.

After what seemed like an hour she finally closed her eyes, took a deep breath, and walked over to the info desk. "Hi. We're supposed to meet someone here. He has tickets for the show that's about to start?"

The man behind the counter looked confused. "Oh...I'm sorry, but it's just sold out."

Ma smiled. "I know. We're guests of..." She glanced around as if she was sort of embarrassed to mention the connection, and then whispered. "My ex-husband is Dr. Arturo Ortega. He reserved seats for us."

"Oh!" The man typed some words into the screen and nodded. "Ah, yes. I see. Unfortunately, those tickets are no longer available."

Ma leaned in, frowning. "I'm sorry...what?"

"I'm afraid Dr. Ortega needed to be here in person, ten minutes before the show, in order to claim those particular seats. So they were given to someone else."

Christina and Javi were staring at the guy as if he'd just said we were not welcome and being kicked out. But I wasn't worried. My father had made special plans for my birthday. As soon as he got here, he'd explain how it was all a misunderstanding. I swallowed my last bite of pretzel and licked a few crumbs of salt from my lips.

The man held a hand up. "Oh, wait a sec. There's a message here for...you're Magda Soto, correct?"

"Yes. I am." Ma's voice was sharp now.

"Dr. Ortega sends his regrets," the man read off the screen. "Says he won't be able to make it after all."

My lips burned. Stupid big, crunchy salt. "Wait. He's not coming?"

The guy cleared his throat. "Good news is, he was able to purchase four standard tickets for a show later this afternoon." He smiled at me. "So, what do you think of that, buddy?"

The man had no clue. The whole point of today, of this entire trip into the city, was so we could see my father in person. For my birthday.

"I don't want to stay."

"We'll pass on the afternoon tickets to someone else. Thanks." Ma hurried us away, past the Barosaurus. "I'm so, so sorry, m'ijo. I'm sure Pa will call you later and explain what happened."

Javi tossed the rest of his pretzel in the trash. "Not cool to leave the little dude hanging, especially today."

Christina huffed. "For once Pa promises to see Ig on his birthday, instead of just a phone call, and he doesn't even bother to show up?" She crossed her arms, scowling. "Tell him he doesn't have to worry about calling me on my birthday anymore. I don't want to speak to him. Ever again."

My stomach turned then, for real. The pretzel was lying like a greasy, salty rock in the bottom of it. And then and there I decided two things: That I'd never eat another soft pretzel again, in my life. And, like my sister, I didn't want to talk to my father, ever again.

# CHAPTER EIGHT:
# SURPRISE GUEST

In the auditorium of the environmental center, it feels like an eternity before I can speak to my father. First I have to push away the memory of that old birthday disappointment.

"Uh...hi." It's all I can manage, because my mind is racing with so many other thoughts.

*Why is he here? Why didn't he tell us he was coming? Why is he so much shorter than I'd imagined?*

"It wasn't definite that I'd be able to make tonight. That's why I didn't mention it in my last postcard." He holds out his arms, but I'm frozen in place. We stand like that for an excruciating moment before he steps in to hug me. Awkwardly. And then quickly steps back.

It all feels so strange. Especially since we're in public and my friends are standing right next to me, staring, completely clueless about what's going on.

Ju narrows her eyes as if to say, *Who is this guy?*

"Do you work here at the observatory?" Gunther asks.

"No. I'm in the field, but my work is, well, global. Arturo Ortega." He reaches for Gunther's hand, and then Ju's. Giving them big, hearty handshakes like he's running for mayor or something. "I can tell you've got some great friends, Ignacio."

"Have we met before?" Ju scrunches her forehead. "You look kind of familiar."

Oh, no. Has she seen him on television? I wish I could fall into a black hole.

Gunther playfully punches my arm. "Why didn't you say you're buddies with a famous science guy, Ig?"

"I guess Ignacio hasn't told you then." Pa clears his throat. "I'm his father."

"Wait, what? His father?" Ju steps back. Her gaze meets mine and she slowly shakes her head. "Oh, sorry. Um, nice to meet you. Excuse me. I have to use the restroom." She bolts up the aisle and into the lobby.

We start walking the same direction, Gunther leading the way. "This is so cool. I mean, your dad's a real-life space genius? Can't beat that."

My friend has no clue how complicated this all is. Or that it's the first time I'm meeting my father in person, or at least the first time I'll be able to remember. And that this seemingly nice surprise feels like I've been betrayed all over again.

At the doorway, my father stands back, letting me and Gunther go through first. The lobby is buzzing with visitors clutching shiny new books, lining up for Dr. Cho's autograph.

"Uh, Gunther," I say. "Mind if I talk with my father alone for a few minutes?"

"Oh. Sure. Of course." He shakes Pa's hand again. "Nice to meet you."

"My pleasure," he says. After Gunther leaves, he adds, "They do seem nice."

I stare at my sneakers, unable to look at him. I'm afraid I might scowl instead of smile back. "Does Ma know you're here?"

"Not yet. I'm going to call her tonight. I want to make plans to see Javier and Christina, too."

I take a deep breath. "I'd only make plans with them if you're actually going to go through with it."

"Of course. That goes without saying." He clears his throat again, as if he's nervous too. "You look good." He lays a hand on my shoulder, but the gesture feels forced. We're like two  mismatched mannequins in a store window. At least mannequins don't have feelings. And I have so many just now, I can't sort them out.

"You should've warned me you were coming," I say at last. "I would've prepared better."

He removes his hand from my shoulder, looking puzzled. "Prepared?"

What a silly thing to say. A moment like this isn't something anyone can prepare for.

"Dr. Ortega?" A blonde woman in a gray suit and heels totters up to us. "Sheila White. I just wanted to let you know I've read your latest research on spiral galaxies. Brilliant, as always. Dr. Nolan advised me to speak with you about your upcoming keynote in Boston."

"I'd be happy to discuss it. Perhaps tomorrow during the networking breakfast?" He smiles and gestures toward me. "Right now I'm catching up with my son."

The woman blinks. She looks at me like I've just appeared out of nowhere. "Oh, my. I didn't realize you had a son."

"Actually, I've got two," he says, sounding proud. "And a daughter."

I wonder if he tells everyone he meets about the three of us.

"What's your name?" The woman leans over , speaking in a higher voice , as if I'm a toddler.

"Ignacio," I say. "From the Latin 'ignis,' meaning fire."

Her eyebrows pop up. "Oh, I see. A real smarty pants. Just like your dad." She smiles at me and then at my father. "I'll look forward to speaking with you tomorrow, then." And she walks away.

"Maybe we should go in here?" He nods, pointing to the insect classroom, a few feet away. I flick on the lights. There are posters of ants, dragonflies, and cicadas as well as glass displays of wasps, hornets, and honeybees. "Hope you're not afraid of bugs."

"Oh, right." He glances around, pushing his glasses up higher on his nose. "The assistant director of the center mentioned they have quite an insect and arachnid collection."

Gunther appears in the doorway. "They're in here!"

My father smiles. "I guess we're just too popular today, huh?"

Gunther sticks his head in and peers around the room "Eew. What kind of sick exhibit is this?" He backs out, bumping into Ju.

Ju rolls her eyes. "Watch it. Uh, my mom's here to pick us up."

"Oh, I..." I glare at my father, who looks kind of sad. "Guess I've got to go."

"Know what?" Pa says. "I've got a car service. I'll see that Ignacio gets home. That way we won't hold you up."

"Car service?" Ju raises her eyebrows as if he just said he's being driven around town on a chariot.

"That's so Hollywood." Gunther smiles.

My father laughs. "The center arranged one for my stay."

My friends say their goodbyes, then turn away and walk off. Part of me wants to run after them. To continue with the night as I'd expected it to go. Maybe come up with a new theory for the telescope mystery on the car ride home. But I can't leave my father now that he's here. I have so many questions for him, so many thoughts, good and bad. Who knows when , of even if, I'll get another chance to ask? Plus, there's still that disappointed little boy in me. The one who ate a soft pretzel while waiting for his father to appear for a planetarium show at the Museum of Natural History, all those years ago. That little boy wants to make the most of this moment now that I finally have my mysterious father all to myself.

"Do you always get driven around?" I blurt out, then want to kick myself. Of all the important questions I have swirling inside, *that's* the one that comes out?

"Not really. But more so, recently." He sits at a microscope station and slides out the chair next to him. "Why don't you take a seat?"

I sit one station over, wondering why he seems so serious all of a sudden.

My father taps a stack of microscope slides of butterfly wings. They seem so fragile underneath his fingers. "The Lenape Environmental Center invited me to be a visiting scientist for the next four weeks."

"Oh." Four weeks? I'm not sure if this is great, or terrible.

He doesn't meet my gaze. "There will be four of us here, doing research and helping the staff upgrade the facilities with new technologies."

"Like what?"

"We'll be working on making several sections of the center fully accessible for people with different abilities," he says.

"Oh. That's good." I nod. "Where do you go when the four weeks are up?"

"I'll head up to Boston with..." Pa hesitates, then smiles and stands up suddenly. He sure is moving around a lot.

"With the other scientists visiting the center?" I ask.

"No...well, yes. What I mean is...." His hand twitches and he knocks over the slides. "Oh, this is not how I wanted...I'm sorry. Guess the jet lag is getting to me." He sits again, this time going really still. "I am traveling with one of the other visiting scientists. In fact, we travel together quite a bit. There's something else you should know, Ignacio." He takes a deep breath. "I'm getting married."

"Married?" I whisper. My heart takes a lurch, then races. Somehow I didn't think it was possible for him to drop an even bigger bombshell on me right now. And yet there it is. Dashing the hope I have held all this time way in the back of my mind. A wish so silly, I couldn't ever admit I'd been holding on to it. That one day my parents would get back together. And we'd be a real family again. Right here in Dolton. Or even somewhere else on earth.

# CHAPTER NINE:
# A CAR RIDE WITH PA

It's a short drive from the observatory to the condo complex where my father and Dr. Lin Cho are being housed. She's sitting in the front passenger seat of the black Lincoln car that smells like fake vanilla. The driver next to her is a tall man with a bushy beard.

*My father is getting married. My father is getting married to Dr. Lin Cho.*

I've repeated these two things countless times since he told me. But somehow that doesn't help. It's still impossible to believe.

Only a half hour ago Pa introduced me to Dr. Cho. Right after the festival had ended, and most of the people had left. She signed my copy of *Collision Course* and then even hugged me after handing it back. That, I didn't expect.

Once we pull up to the entrance of the condo complex of white brick buildings, Dr. Cho turns toward the back seat to look at me. Her smooth dark hair is neatly tucked under a pink beret. "I'm so happy I was able to meet you tonight, Ignacio. I look forward to seeing you again, later in the week."

"Yeah." I swallow hard, still trying to make sense of anything that's happened tonight. "Thanks for signing my book."

She smiles widely and then turns to glance at my father, who is seated next to me in the back. "See you in a bit, Artie." The car door creaks open, and she lets herself out, disappearing into the front door of the fancy condo complex.

Artie? Ugh. What an awful nickname. I kind of want to hold that against Dr. Cho as proof that she's lame, but in fact she's nice and super smart. Still...she's not Ma.

"Should take about ten minutes to get to this address in Dolton," the driver says, pulling out of the parking lot.

"Excellent." Pa stares over at me for what feels like an eternity. "Lin seems to like you."

"I guess." I'm also guessing that now I'm supposed to say I like her too, but I just can't. I mean, I don't really know her, do I?

"Two of the most important people in my life, meeting for the first time. At last. Made me happy to see it." He pats the arm of my coat.

I shift in the seat.

He clears his throat, and the smile fades. "What's wrong?"

It must seem like I'm trying to move away from him. Am I? Maybe so. It's not like I want to rob him of his happiness or anything. But I can't just pretend like everything that happened today is normal and fine. I wish he'd just think about what this news would feel like for...well, anyone who's not him.

I shrug. "Maybe I haven't gotten over the shock yet."

"Did I shock you?" He frowns.

"Kind of."

"Oh." He exhales loudly. "Sorry about that. Guess I was so excited, I moved a bit too fast."

I stare out the window as we pass a brightly-lit playground. The place looks strange at night with no kids on the swings or slide. Like a set made for a movie or something. I try to imagine what it would've been like to run around on a playground like it, with my father watching, when I was little. Would he have pushed me high in the swings? Caught me at the bottom of the slide?

Our car turns onto the main street in town, approaching the train tracks just as the red and white striped barrier lowers, lights flashing. The car slows to a stop.

"Commuter train." The driver uses the rearview mirror to glance back at both of us. "Shouldn't be too long."

*Thank goodness.* The second the thought crosses my mind I feel awful. I should be grateful to be sitting next to my father. Even if he did surprise me.

Outside, past a small courtyard in front of the public library, several high school guys are hanging around. Some are riding skateboards. One flies up on the railing, then soars over an entire set of steps, somehow still landing upright on the sidewalk. A friend runs up to him, and they bump chests in mid-air. The others yell and high-five each other. Their celebrating reminds me of old videos I've seen of NASA's mission control after a successful shuttle or rocket launch.

"Haven't seen a reaction like that since NASA landed that rocket on the aircraft carrier in the middle of the ocean," my father says, gazing out at the teenagers.

I gape at him. "I thought about NASA just then, too!"

"Great minds think alike." He winks.

I feel my face flush hot. Is there some alternate universe where he's been around for my entire childhood, the two of us there doing stuff like comparing things to NASA, as if it's a fact of life, something I could take for granted?

The train gate lifts and the car starts moving again. As we pull away from the library, I spot another guy outside, leaning on a light pole. The same one who was inside the gazebo the other day when Ju and I stopped there on the way home. Same green army coat, same long blond hair in a ponytail. He only gives a thumbs up to the other celebrating skaters from where he stands. Somehow part of the group, but also apart from them.

We turn off the main road, leaving the skateboarders behind. Soon enough we're pulling into the narrow driveway of our three-family house. I open the back door on the passenger side carefully, so I don't hit the chain link fence and scratch the paint.

The driver holds open the door for my father on the opposite side. "Tight squeeze with this fence, Dr. Ortega. A bit dark, but the sidewalk and front stoop are well lit."

The driver seems really attentive, or maybe just nervous about doing a good job driving a famous scientist around.

'Thank you," my father tells him. "I'll probably be here an hour or so."

"I'll be back by then." The driver nods and gets back into the car.

It's kind of strange to see my father being treated like royalty, but I guess he's used to going to fancy places, in fancy cars, all over the world.

Pa pauses at the bottom of the steps. He peers up, pushing his glasses higher onto his nose. "So this is your home."

"The first floor is ours," I tell him. Little Cory is already barking his head off from the apartment above. "The Milcus are on the second level. Tangas on the third. We all share the basement and the roof."

"Oh. A flat roof?" He sounds intrigued.

"Yeah, it is." I unlock the door to the lobby and hold it open for him. "Spend a lot of time up there with my binoculars. On a clear night, I can see Vega and Jupiter."

I reach out for the knob of the inside door to our apartment, but it swings open before I can get my key in the lock. Ma stands there in her nurse scrubs, staring out at my father.

"Magda." He nods. "Uh, hi." He sounds nervous.

"Arturo." She steps back. "Come in."

He slowly shuffles into our apartment, which tonight smells like Ma's chicken soup.

She smiles at me. "Did you have fun at the festival, Ignacio?"

"Yeah."

"Good." She clasps her hands together as if she's nervous, too, and doesn't want anyone to see them tremble.

And then it's quiet. Too quiet, really. Even the Yorkie upstairs must feel how tense it is right through the ceiling, because finally he's stopped yapping.

My father glances down the dim, narrow hallway. "Where are Javier and Christina?"

"Out." Ma closes the door and leans back against it. "He took the mini-van. Last minute plans. And Christina...I don't know where she's gone off to."

"Oh. I see." He looks down, and presses his lips together. "Too bad. Was hoping to see them, too."

"Yes, well..." She crosses her arms that firm way she does when one of us has misbehaved. "Things don't always work out the way you'd like, I guess."

I hang my jacket on one of the hooks, and then hold out a hand. "Um...can I hang up your coat?"

"Thank you, Ignacio." My father slips out of his long black wool coat.

Ma stares at his feet. "Still wearing sneakers with a suit jacket after all these years."

He follows her into the living room, pausing to look at the Cuban painting above the sofa. "I remember this piece. The faceless children always scared Christina."

69

"Hmph. She's over it now." She turns to me. "Hungry, mi amor?"

"A little," I say, nodding.

"You're welcome to have some soup as well, Arturo."

"Oh. No, thanks." Then he probably worries Ma's feeling insulted, because he quickly adds, "I'm sure the dinner is wonderful, but I already ate."

"Okay then." She tilts her head. "Un cafecito at least?"

"Decaf? Don't want to be up too late. I've got an early networking breakfast."

"Decaf it is." She clears her throat and crosses the hall into the kitchen.

My father sighs then, as if he's preparing for battle, and follows after her.

# CHAPTER TEN:
# UNFAMILIAR HOME

Fifteen minutes later I sling my backpack over the top of a kitchen chair and sit down in front of a bowl of hot chicken soup. My father sits across from me, staring around at the red-orange walls, holding my Mercury mug. It's steaming with fresh decaf coffee. "Quite a color scheme in here."

"Ma chose the colors."

"To remind me of back home." She sips some coffee but doesn't look up.

Both of my parents were born in Cuba. They immigrated to the states as kids, and met in Miami as teens, in high school.

"Well, to each his own." My father nervously taps the side of the mug with one long finger.

Ma's eyebrows shoot up. "Or *her* own?"

My father turns at last to look her in the eye. "Of course. I stand corrected. Look, Magda...I'm not here to argue." His face flushes. "I only want to...well, first I want to make sure the kids understand. I mean, do they know I wanted to take you all with me? To keep the family together. To show them the world."

She frowns. "They needed stability. Not a childhood of hotel rooms and never-ending vacations."

"What better way to learn than by being exposed to all sorts of cultures, languages, and environments? You'd be amazed at the excellent homeschooling programs out there." Pa sets the mug down a little too hard, and some coffee sloshes out onto the table.

Ma leans across and uses a paper napkin to mop up the spill. "So, what...are you trying to convince me all over again?"

"It wasn't only about my career," he says. "I thought of the kids' education, too."

She snorts. "Really? And what about me? Ever think I might have wanted a career, too?"

He opens his mouth, but nothing comes out. Instead, he stands abruptly, takes a few steps away, facing the colorful wall again. Ma's still in her chair, arms crossed, eyes now closed.

I'm finally in the same room with both my parents. Something I've dreamed about for so many years. But in my dream, Javi and Christina are here too. We're all eating a big meal together, and everyone is laughing.

Pa removes his glasses and sighs. "Ignacio, would you mind giving us a little privacy?"

My mother purses her lips. She slides a tray out from a cabinet and sets my bowl on it, with a napkin. "You have permission to eat in your room, papito."

Now I know she means business because we're never allowed to have meals in our rooms. I throw my backpack over one shoulder and carry the tray down the narrow hall. Before I step into my bedroom, I hear my father say softly. "You're right, Magda."

I flick on the switch, toss my backpack on the floor, and close the door. I still hear angry voices, but they're muffled now. And you know what? I don't want to know what they're saying. I'd rather think about something else. Something other than my mother and father acting like they've stepped in a boxing ring, ready for a fight.

I spot my casebook wedged between my bed and the wall. I wonder if Gunther and Ju came up with any new theories on the ride home. Then again, Ju might have been too shocked by meeting my father to focus on the investigation. I hope she isn't upset that I never told her how I knew him . . . or at least that I knew of him . . . before today. Maybe I should call her. But what would I say?

No. I've had enough drama for one night. The safest thing to think about?

The case. Yes, I'd much rather do that.

I set the tray on my tiny desk to let the soup cool down a bit. Then grab a pen and fall into bed to update the latest data.

*OBSERVATION:*
*There's a strange red light that appears in a single photo taken inside the observatory on the night of the incident.*

*~~HYPOTHESIS~~: PROVEN FALSE*
*~~One of the college interns (Julissa or Jalani) caused the telescope to move.~~*

*DATA:*
*Witness testimony: Oliver Pontmercy, the security guard, reported that security videos taken inside the observatory cleared both of the interns.*

*RESEARCH:*
*The strange red light was labeled ACCESS.*

Once I'm done with the case notes. I slide *Collision Course* out of my backpack and flip to the front. The scrawl of hot pink ink inside, on the title page, reads:

Ignacio,
Keep looking up.

Dr. Cho's signature is below that, in fat bubbly letters.

As I close the cover, there's a knock at the door.

"Ignacio," my father calls in a soft voice.

I drop the casebook on my bed and open the door. "Hey."

"Thank you for giving us some privacy," he says.

"No problem." I step back. "Want to see my room?"

"Of course." He steps in and turns around, taking it in.

"It's small, I know, but..."

"No, it's great." He looks at my wall display. "These are all my articles?"

I nod. "I'm pretty sure I got them all."

"Wow." He clears his throat. "What're you marking on this map?"

"There's a pin for each postcard you send. Probably near fifty by now." *Does he even know the number,* I wonder. "I keep track of them. Reminds me of all the places I'd like to visit someday."

He lifts my binoculars and hefts them up and down as if he's memorized the model by weight. "The Galactic Skyscape." He smiles. "It's a great pair for the beginner astronomer."

"Want to go to the roof and check them out?"

"Oh well, I'd love to, but...." Pa hands back the binoculars. "The driver should be here any minute. I'll see you later this week, though, okay?" He ruffles my hair. "I promise."

He leaves, closing the door softly behind him.

I hope he keeps that promise. Because as much drama as he's brought into my life, I still want to look at the stars with my father.

An hour later I'm in our narrow hallway putting the binoculars around my neck, making sure the collar of my coat doesn't trap the strap. I hear Ma pacing like a hungry lion on the other side of the wall in the living room. I step into the doorway.

She's clutching the landline phone to her ear and waving around a crumpled tissue. "Pero, Sonia, how would that have looked to Ignacio? I had to let Arturo inside," Ma says to my aunt. "Anyway, I wanted to hear what he had to say for himself." She stops talking and stands still, listening. Then she shakes her head and then lets it fall forward. "Of course not. I didn't expect him to say *that.*"

Ma's shoulders slump forward, and she exhales as if exhausted. She doesn't look like her usual self, strong and confident. She looks small and very tired. I want to put my arms around her, but then she'd know I was listening in to her conversation. She absolutely hates eavesdropping. And, well, I'd definitely be guilty as charged.

She sniffs and wipes her eyes with the tissue. "It was the right thing to do, though, wasn't it?"

I slide back far enough so she won't see me. I should just quietly walk into the kitchen and up the back stairwell onto the roof. Instead, my feet stay glued in place. How can I move when I've just seen my mother look so deflated and unsure of herself? But then, how else did I think she'd feel? Based on this reaction, she's just found out my father is getting married and starting a new life without us. It only makes sense that it's messing with her mind.

"Gracias, Sonia," Ma whispers, and then hangs up the phone. She sniffles again, and sighs.

I count to ten before I walk into the living room.

By then Ma's nose is buried in one of her nursing schoolbooks. She glances up, eyes still red. "Hey, how you doing, m'ijo?"

"Okay." I shrug. "Fine."

She leans her head back on the sofa. "You must be feeling all kinds of emotions about this surprise visit. You want to talk about it?" She gets up and rests a hand on my arm. "Go ahead. Tell me."

"I wish he could make a promise and stick to it, and..." I look down at my binoculars because I can't quite meet her eyes. "And not bail. Or not show up with no warning."

She nods slowly. "When you don't know what to expect from someone, it's hard to decide where you really stand. That's one reason why I always wanted you, Javi, and Christina to have stability. A routine you could count on. But your father...well, as you know, he has a different perspective." She holds me at arm's length. Her eyes look watery, but she's not exactly crying. "I'm proud of how you handled this. Javier and Christina are still struggling with their anger."

Anger. Is that what I'm feeling? "Can't blame them though. I mean...."

She studies my face. "You're angry, too."

I let out a held breath. "I get how they feel. Like when I think about how Pa doesn't know even the simplest things about us. I mean, he just saw my bedroom and my postcard map for the first time ever. It seems wrong. And unfair. I want him to know everything he's missed out on."

She gently tugs at my hair. "Maybe you can help him understand that while he's here."

"Maybe." I clear my throat. "Anyhow... I'll be on the roof."

Ma smiles and returns to the couch, and to her book. "Enjoy the stars, mi amor."

# CHAPTER ELEVEN:
# KEEP LOOKING UP

The back stairwell smells like a combo of Ma's soup and the chocolate rice porridge the Tangas sometimes make. I take the stairs two at a time until I reach the top floor. The strong beat of a hip-hop song grows louder with each step. The neighbors on the street behind us are always throwing loud weekend parties, cranking up the music. I push hard against the heavy steel door leading out into the cold. Wind slaps my face like a pair of frozen hands. A gust so strong, the huge rooftop air conditioning vent creaks.

I peer up at the sky and sigh. Thick cloud cover. I should've checked visibility on the Night SkyCaster website.

I take a few steps toward the tall brick barrier of the roof, trying to catch a glimpse of the neighbors' party. A couple of people stand on the fire escape, smoking. Behind curtained windows, shadows move in time to the deep bass rhythm. It looks pretty amazing, a party from a distance. Like a galaxy of happiness.

It reminds me of spending Thanksgiving at my aunt Sonia's apartment with my cousins Nilda and Freddie. Nilda's a year older than me and obsessed with her pug dog, Desi Arnaz. Freddie's the same age as Javi. These days he goes by the name DJ Woke. Hard to believe Thanksgiving's only a week and a half away.

I hear a muffled sob near the huge rooftop air conditioning vent. Followed by a sniffle. Both sound familiar.

"Christina?"

"I didn't want to see him." She's a dark shape huddled in the nearest corner. "I kept thinking of how he stood you up at the museum when you were just a little squirt, and I ...I couldn't..."

I walk over to where she's leaning against the vent. "Know what was crazy? I was thinking of that day at the museum before I even knew he was here. Because they were selling soft pretzels at the center. That combined smell of hot yeasty dough and the big crunchy flakes of salt always reminds me of how sad Ma looked that day when the guy behind the counter told her Pa wasn't coming."

Christina wipes her eyes. "I hate those pretzels."

"Me too. Never ate another one after that day."

She shivers. "How dare he drop by like this, with no warning. Did he think that by surprising us, we'd somehow forget all he's done wrong? That we'd instantly become his happy kids?"

I sigh. "I was with my friends, and he just appeared. I didn't know what to say."

She pulls back the hood of her winter coat. "Me, I would've run out of the building."

"I thought about it for a second. But then..." I sit on the bench. "I wanted to see what he's like in person. I was so little when...I don't remember him like you and Javi do. I mean, he's still our father, so – "

"Yeah." Christina crosses her arms. "Well, I don't want to see him." She throws her head back and takes a deep breath. "Smells like it's going to snow."

I tap my binoculars. "Yeah. Those snow clouds ruined my plans."

"Weren't you at the observatory before? How much looking at the stars can a guy do in one night?"

"A lot! You know, there's this Astronomy Camp in Arizona in the middle of the desert. You can stay up overnight. They even give you a midnight snack."

"Nice." She nods. "So it doesn't just ruin your sleep, but your regular meals, too."

I shrug. "Ma works night shifts, doesn't she?"

"It's her job, you dork."

"Well, someday my job will be night work, too. Hopefully, doing research on a telescope in the Chilean desert or on a Hawaiian island."

She stares at me. "You want to be just like him."

81

"Not really." True, I wonder what it'd be like to travel to all those places in the postcards he's sent. That doesn't mean I want to act like him. Not if it means canceling plans and surprise visits. Not if it means disappointing my family, over and over.

"I want to see the sky from other parts of the world. I want to keep looking up, that's all." But I know explaining this for the millionth time won't make my sister understand it any better.

Christina sniffs again. "That iPod I gave you still work?"

"Yeah." She gave me her old one last year since I'm not allowed to have a cell phone. The main reason I wanted it was to listen to the *Celestial Stuff* podcast.

"Still listening to that nerdy space show?" Christina shoves her bare hands into her pockets and shivers.

I wiggled my gloved fingers, thankful that I remembered to put them on. "Every week."

She looks down at her knees. "He was on an episode one time, wasn't he?"

"Pa? He's been it on a bunch." For all her talk about not wanting anything to do with my father, she sure seems interested in learning about him. "The most recent one's about exoplanets."

"Exoplanets?" She laughs. "Sounds like some kind of shellfish on a menu."

"They're planets found orbiting another sun," I explain.

She bumps her shoulder into mine. "You're pretty smart, dork."

I grin. "Thanks."

From Christina, that's a big-time compliment. And honestly, it means a lot to hear her say it. Not that I'd ever tell her so.

# CHAPTER TWELVE:
# NOMINATIONS

Javi steers the car off the street and into the drop-off zone in front of Dolton Middle School. I've been trying to find a way to ask him something the whole car ride over. It almost seems harder to bring up my father to him than it was to discuss him with Christina last night, on the roof.

"Uh, bro, you getting out sometime this year?" Javi fiddles with the temperature knob. The fan rattles and heat streams with even more force from the vents. "The later I get to campus, the harder it is to find a parking spot."

"You're going to see him before he leaves, right?"

"Who?"

"Pa. I mean, you've got some time now, since he's one of the visiting scientists."

Javi sniffs. "Don't worry about me, 'kay?"

"Thanks for the ride." I yank the handle and jump out the open door. Soon as I slam it shut behind me. Javi quickly drives away, as if he's worried I'll ask him again.

It's not such a long walk to the front door of the building, but it's snowing hard out. I hang my backpack over both shoulders this time, for balance, and start off, walking carefully on the icy spots.

Then I hear Gunther shouting at me.

"Soto!" He rushes up the sidewalk, panting, face a deep shade of wind-chafed pink.

"Hi, Gunth."

"Saturday was the best, dude." He raises both hands in the air, in two gloved fists.

A teacher's aide holds the door to the main entrance open. "Better hurry up, boys," she calls. "Don't want to be late."

"But why didn't you clue us in about your father being a big shot scientist?" Gunther says as we approach our lockers.

"Hey, *guys!*" Elijah runs up, furiously waving a paper above his purple L.A. Lakers winter hat. "Don't forget *nominations* for the Choose Your Field Trip contest are due by the end of school today."

"Oh yeah." Gunther sticks a hand into the front pocket of his backpack and yanks out a wrinkled sheet of paper . He holds it up triumphantly, like it's a wad of cash. "Here it is."

"Oh, yeah. That's right." I'd forgotten about the contest with all that's been going on with my father and the mysterious telescope case. There sure is a lot to think about today. But there's no way I'd pass up nominating the observatory for the spring field trip.

By noon, I'm eager to get to lunch so I can fill out my form and turn it in before the deadline. When I rush by Mr. Orin's classroom, he's teetering up on a chair, wrestling with a rolled poster that keeps curling in on itself as he tries to tack it up onto the wall.

I stop in the doorway. "Um, need any help, Mr. Orin?"

He glances down at me from under one arm. "Ignacio! Perfect timing. If you could hold this bottom corner in place, that'd be fantastic."

I do as he says. After a minute or so, he secures all four corners and climbs down to survey his work. "Thank goodness it's straight!"

I stare at the poster, which shows all the cloud types. Stratus, long and flat. Cumulus, white and puffy. Cirrus, light and wispy. "Ugh, it's all just clouds."

Mr. Orin laughs. "What, not a fan?"

I shrug. "It's just that they get in the way of viewing stars and stuff at night."

"Ah, I see." He nods. "I suppose any fan of stargazing would be less than enthusiastic about overcast days. But clouds do help make life as we know it possible, so we can't hate them too much."

"Of course." I smile. "I mean, they're fine during daylight hours."

He laughs. "You know, Gunther mentioned to me that he met your father at the environmental center this weekend."

"Oh." I look down at my feet. My cheeks get very hot. "Um, yeah."

He clears his throat. "I'm curious as to why you never brought up in class that you were related to the famous Dr. Ortega."

Is the whole universe conspiring to tell me to stop being so secretive about my elusive father? I shrug. "Dunno. I'm kind of a private person, I guess."

"Fair enough." He returns the chair to one of the student desks. "Did you enjoy the festival?"

"Of course. I love the center."

He smiles. "That's good to hear. Thanks for helping with the poster."

"You're welcome. Now I better get to lunch." I rush out into the almost empty hallway just as the warning bell rings.

I run down the hall so fast I almost don't see Ju standing in the outer area of the nurse's suite, head down, gazing at the floor. The bell for the next period rings. Good thing I'm on my way to lunch, so it won't count against me when I show up late.

There are two cots in the nurse's suite. A big corkboard with several nutrition posters hangs on the wall behind a couple of small upholstered chairs. I double back and stick my head in the doorway. "Hey."

Ju looks up. "Oh. Hi." She half-smiles and tucks her curly hair behind her ears.

"What happened?"

She's got a Band-Aid on her pinky finger. "Caught it on a sharp edge of my locker door."

"Ouch. That stinks."

"It stopped bleeding. Nothing too major." She points at the closed door of the inner office, which has a frosted window. "The nurse is busy right now. A puking sixth grader."

"I'm not here to see her." I sit on a cot. "Just noticed you sitting in here."

She sighs. "I guess now I know how you felt when I didn't tell you what was going on with my family last month." She comes over and sits on the cot across from me. "Did you know he was coming?"

"Not at all." I take a deep breath and slowly let it out. "That was the first time I'd seen my father since I was a baby. In fact, I have no memory of ever meeting him."

She narrows her eyes. "You really didn't have any contact all these years?"

"We used to speak on the phone, up until my sixth birthday. And then...." I tell her the story about the day he never showed up at the museum in New York City.

"Oh," she says, softly. "Wow. The articles and postcards on your walls...."

"He sends me postcards from lots of places, and pays for stuff." I lean my elbows on my knees. "He's just not...around. He's too busy being Dr. Arturo Ortega, Science Superstar."

"I can't imagine seeing my father all over the place, like a celebrity, but not actually...seeing him." She pulls up her knees and hugs them to her chest, looking sad for me.

I shrug. "In a way, I'm used to all that." I softly punch the pillow. "But he did tell me something the other day that's kind of, um, well...okay. I'll just go ahead and say it. Remember Dr. Cho? My father's marrying her soon."

Her jaw drops. "Wow. You had lots of big surprises on Saturday night."

I nod. "Oh yeah."

The door to the nurse's inner office creaks opens. The combined scents of bleach and alcohol vapors waft into the outer area. Mrs. Abu ushers out a tall eighth-grade girl who is squinting hard even though it's not all that bright in the room.

"If the migraine doesn't subside within the hour, Alissa, I'll call your parents," the nurse says in a soft voice.

Wincing, a hand shading her eyes, the eighth-grader shuffles out into the hallway.

Mrs. Abu turns to us and smiles. "What's ailing you today, Ignacio?"

I stand. "No ailments, Mrs. Abu. We're just on our way to lunch."

Ju holds up the bandaged finger as she bounces up from her chair. "I'm good now. Thanks for the Band-Aid!"

Mrs. Abu nods, adjusting her headscarf. "Enjoy your meal, you two. Smells like fish sticks today." She hums on her way back into her office. Ju and I step out into the hallway together, headed for the cafeteria.

89

Gunther's done eating his lunch by the time we finally get there. "What took you guys so long?" His tray is pushed aside, and he's hunched over the field trip nomination form.

Ju slides her recycled nylon lunch bag onto the table. "I was at the nurse's office getting a Band-Aid. Cut my finger."

I set my tray down. Fish sticks and soggy fries. But lots of ketchup makes them taste okay.

"We've only got until the end of today to get our forms in." Gunther taps his with a pointer finger, like he's lecturing us. "We should go for the ultimate adventure. The big Kahuna. Got nothing to lose."

Ju and I glance at each other. "What in the world are you talking about?" she asks.

Gunther slides the Lenape Environmental Center's field trip brochure across the table. He's circled the description for the Science Slumber Party. "I think the entire seventh grade should go to the Science Slumber Party at the environmental center."

Ju props both hands on her hips, looking incredulous. "You really think the school would go for an overnight trip? I mean, it'd have to be on a weekend, for starters."

I think Gunter is on to something. Why not dream big? I drag the blank nomination form from my backpack. "Sure. We just have to make a case they can't refuse."

Dolton Middle School
CHOOSE YOUR FIELD TRIP CONTEST
Nomination Form

Name: Ignacio Soto
Nomination: Lenape Environmental Center
(Science Slumber Party)
The next seventh grade field trip should be
to the Lenape Environmental Center,
because it has the Sloan Observatory where
students can view celestial objects like
planets, star clusters, and the moon. A lot of
middle school students have probably never
looked through a professional telescope
before, so that will be a unique educational
experience. We can also walk on the Jersey
Devil Trails and do science experiments in
the Barton Biosphere.

Dolton Middle School
CHOOSE YOUR FIELD TRIP CONTEST
Nomination Form

Name: Gunther Corrie
Nomination: Lenape Environmental Center (Science Slumber Party)
My favorite part of the Lenape Environmental Center is the Jersey
Devil Trail. It's got a bunch of colorful birdhouses, an overlook where
you can view New York City, and an awesome amphitheater (an outdoor

91

stage that has big rocks for seats). The Science Slumber Party also includes the awesome Barton Biosphere and the Sloan Observatory - and the whole thing comes with pizza!

## Dolton Middle School
## CHOOSE YOUR FIELD TRIP CONTEST
## Nomination Form

Name: Justina Feliciano

Nomination: Lenape Environmental Center (Science Slumber Party)

It's a cold hard fact that the seventh graders of Dolton Middle School could really learn a lot about nature by choosing the Lenape Environmental Center for our next field trip. I especially like the Barton Biosphere because it has scientific exhibits about animals and plants. There's even a room with microscopes that allow you to look closely at things like bug antennae and dust mites. We can also use the Sloan Observatory and the Jersey Devil Trails to learn even more. And the park is only a couple towns away, so it's convenient, too.

# THROWBACK: SIXTH GRADE DISAPPEARING SOUNDS

For last year's field trip, in sixth grade, we went to the Thomas Edison National Park just like every sixth-grade class at Dolton Middle School before ours had done.

We'd filed into Edison's former library on the ground floor of his old lab, led by a tall female park ranger with a high-pitched voice. As we toured Edison's old laboratory, I remember thinking he must've invented some kind of potion that made him superhuman. How else could one man have accomplished so much in a single lifetime?

The park ranger explained Edison's daily schedule. She pointed out his desk, a soaring multi-floor library that held thousands of books, and a narrow cot behind a waist-high clear plastic barrier that kept visitors from wandering near or sitting on it. "Edison was known to keep very long work hours, but he also knew the importance of recharging the mind. He took frequent naps on this cot."

"You think he read all these books?" Ju had whispered, staring in awe at the three-story tall bookshelves. "Maybe he had to take naps during the day so he could stay up all night reading."

I pointed at a white marble statue holding up an old-fashioned light bulb with visible filaments. "Sure. Using his snazzy new invention to light the pages."

When the park ranger led us into the music room, though, it felt different. There were several old-fashioned phonographs. Their speakers were large horns that flared out, shaped sort of like big flowers. Some of them played music on cylinders, some on thick old records. Most of the laboratory rooms had been used for building or for experimenting. This space was for just listening.

The ranger played a record on one of the phonographs. An old-timey tune with lots of trumpets and other horns that sounded faint and super-scratchy. Also, the singer sounded kind of goofy, like maybe he had a cold, or was holding his nose while he sang. It wasn't like any music I had ever listened to before. And it was about fruit.

*Yes! We have no bananas*
*We have-a no bananas today*

"Edison was hard of hearing, a detail that's often not mentioned in the classroom," the ranger said. "Of course, he never let hearing loss stand in the way of his work. In fact, he claimed it shut out the noise, and that helped him concentrate."

It made sense to me. My mind was always clearest when I was alone, in silence, staring up at the night sky.

I slipped a hand into my pocket, where I had the latest postcard my father had sent me: Cape Town, South Africa. I'd tried to imagine him along on the field trip with us, instead of on the other side of the world. In my mind, he was doing things like counting kids every hour and making sure it was safe to cross the street, like a regular parent. But I knew he really had more in common with Edison – work always came first.

# CHAPTER THIRTEEN: MEETING AT JU'S

On Saturday afternoon, I ring the bell at Ju's house. Mrs. Feliciano opens the front door and smiles at me. Her dark hair's tied up with a piece of blue yarn. She's wearing a smock with flecks of paint on it. She has a home business making handcrafted clothing and jewelry in her basement studio.

"Hi, Ignacio." She waves me inside. "They're in the den. Can I take your coat?"

"Thanks." I stuff my hat and gloves into one sleeve and hand it to her.

"Ig!" Ju's little sister, Delilah, runs up to me holding out her favorite doll. It looks like a miniature version of her. "Delilah Juniorette invites you to tea." Lah curtsies and her long brown braid flops forward.

Mrs. Feliciano pats her on the shoulder. "Sweetie, he's here for an official meeting. You remember Justina's mystery club."

"Right. But thanks for the invitation, Lah," I say.

"Know what? I need a break from working in the studio." Mrs. Feliciano takes off her smock and hangs it on a hook on the wall. "Delilah, let's play Tea Time in your room."

"Tea, tea, for Mami and me!" Lah squeals, hopping around the foyer.

Mrs. Feliciano winks at me. "Enjoy."

When I step into the den, Ju is seated in a desk office chair, tapping her pen on her open casebook.

Gunther is parked on the red sofa. "What's up, Soto?"

"Hey, guys." I join him on the sofa.

"Hi, Ig." Ju swivels left to right, then back to face the computer screen. "So I found out the cost of that big fancy telescope. Holy cow, the thing's expensive! No wonder Dr. Nolan and Kamir are freaking out!"

She taps the pen against her casebook again. "The college interns have been cleared. Next logical suspects to consider would have to be the evening observatory staff."

I frown. "I just don't see Kamir or Dr. Nolan intentionally doing something like this, though. I wouldn't even put them on the suspect list."

Ju turns to me. "We're serious detectives, Ig. We have to be thorough. To consider all the cold hard facts. So, at least at first, everyone's a suspect."

"Remember , Feliciano pretty much solved our last case, single handed." Gunther taps his tablet with one finger.

"True." I open my notebook and turn to the page with our most recent notes.

"Hmm." Ju tosses her long curly hair over one shoulder. "So, what do we know about Kamir?"

"He's a research assistant, plus he also handles some tech stuff. Like running the program that controls all the tech inside at the observation dome. He's working on research for his PhD," I say.

Ju rubs her chin. "He gets along with Dr. Nolan. Would he maybe be looking to work his way up at the center?"

"Um." I shake my head. "This isn't the school's drama club, Ju. No jealous understudy waiting in the wings."

"How about Dr. Joanne Nolan?" Gunther asks. "What's her deal?"

"She was a professor at Garden State College for ten years," I say. "Then she came to the center when it opened four years ago. Back then, the astronomy section was only in the planning stages."

Ju raises both eyebrows. "You know an awful lot about Dr. Nolan."

"I spend a lot of time at that observatory." I shrug. "Again, no clear motive with her. Just a scientist who loves to share what she knows about outer space."

Gunther narrows his eyes. "What about the security guard?"

"Maybe we should look into that too." I stand abruptly. "The observatory will be open tonight. Who's up for a visit?"

"I'm having dinner with Allie and my bio dad. Can't miss that." Ju sighs and pushes a mass of curly hair out of her eyes. "You two will have to go without me."

I look at Gunther. "Meet tonight after dinner, then? Javi can probably drive us over."

He grins. "Sounds like a plan, Soto."

_HYPOTHESIS:_
One of the members of the evening staff (Dr. Joanne Nolan, Kamir Fitzgerald, or Oliver Pontmercy) caused the telescope to move on its own.

# CHAPTER FOURTEEN:
# VISITING SCIENTISTS

About five hours later, Javi pulls up to the entrance at the environmental center. Oliver walks from the security booth up to the car. "Nice clear night for viewing." He hands us a parking pass and then returns to the booth to push the button that raises the gate.

We pass the electronic sign that now reads:

Lenape Environmental Center
Welcomes Visiting Scientists:.
Lin Cho, Kenneth Jennings, Arturo Ortega, Noreen
Feinstein

"Huh. Visiting scientist." Javi glances at me in the rearview mirror. "That's what you were saying the other day, little bro."

"They're coming to conduct research at the facility for the next few weeks," I say.

Javi huffs. "Oh yeah? He's actually going to stick around that long?"

"Yeah." I nod. "He's staying in those condos up on that hill, just off the highway."

"Nice." Gunther whistles. "I've seen those places."

Javi pulls alongside the entrance to the astronomy wing. "I'll pick you up at nine."

There are still a few minutes left before seven o'clock though. We jump out of the minivan and head inside. In the wide main hallway, a group waits for Dr. Nolan and Kamir to start the Cosmic Night viewing session.

Gunther gazes past me to Dr. Nolan's office, a small room at the end of the astronomy hall, right next to a water fountain. The door to the office is open a crack. "Uh...hey, Ig? I'm kind of thirsty. Let's get a drink at the fountain."

If anyone in the office didn't want their discussion overheard, then surely they'd have closed the door all the way. We both take our time drinking lots of water. Then continue to stand there, staring in fascination at the six-inch-wide hunk of meteor encased in glass a few steps away from the classroom where Dr. Nolan and Kamir are talking.

Gradually I can make out bits and pieces of their conversation.

"And I just confirmed that there's no damage at all," Kamir assures Dr. Nolan.

"Thank goodness." She sounds relieved. Then her tone changes to worry. "But word will get out. The last thing our funders want to see is bad reviews of the center on social media."

"I checked against the latest usage logs, and it matches up," Kamir says.

Then there's some scraping around a moving of chair legs and the rustle of paper, so I miss some of his words.

The next part of his answer I can make out is, "I'm just glad we know the probable cause..."

Usage logs. Why does that sound familiar? Oh, right. Ju knocked over some of those when we were here last week. But what were they for?

"Please let security know about the cause. Tell them to be very discreet about this." Dr. Nolan clears her throat. "We're lucky to have these prominent scientists here doing their research. I'm sure there was no actual intent to cause this."

"Of course," Kamir says. "We don't want to make anyone feel like we're *blaming* them."

Gunther and I glance at each other, mouths open. His face looks as shocked as I feel. *They actually suspect one of the visiting scientists!*

I tug Gunther's coat sleeve, press a finger to my lips and point to an empty corner adjacent to the astronomy wing. We don't speak until we have managed to tiptoe over to a display of bog plants near the locked entrance of the BioSphere.

"There goes Ju's theory about the staff member." Gunther shakes his head and opens the case of his iPad.

"Forget that." I flap both hands in the air frantically. "Do you realize what this means?"

"Oh man, Soto." Gunther's eyes grow wide. "Do you think it could've been your own father? That we're actually investigating him?"

I gulp down a breath, and it seems to stick halfway, like a rock. Then I realize it *couldn't* be my father. "No. That doesn't make any sense. The incident happened the week before the festival while he was still in Europe. He didn't arrive until that night." That's about as strong an alibi as you can have.

Gunther shrugs. "Maybe we should just ask Kamir or Dr. Nolan which of the scientists they think it is."

I shake my head. "You heard them. They don't want anyone to know. Including us. That means, even if we do find out who did it, we've got to keep this between the members of the club. We've got to do this with professional integrity, the way real detectives would."

"Yeah. You're right." Gunther leans against the wall, fingers flying as he shifts images around in the app. "Better get all this new info down while it's fresh in our heads."

I pull my casebook out from my coat pocket. Time to log data for further analysis. That's what I tell myself, while my stomach flip-flops, as I write Dr. Cho's name.

HYPOTHESIS: PROVEN FALSE

*One of the members of the evening staff (Dr. Joanne Nolan, Kamir Fitzgerald, or Oliver Pontmercy) caused the telescope to move.*

*DATA:*
*J. Nolan and K. Fitzgerald know that one of the visiting scientists caused the telescope to move on its own.*

As we line up to climb the steps up into the dome for public viewing session, my mind races, turning over this new information. Which one of the visiting scientists could it be?

On the wall, next to the entrance, I spot a sign that reads:

START UP AND SHUT DOWN PROTOCOL FOR A24

A24. Where do I know that number from?

Oh, right. A24 is short for Andromeda 24-inch Series! Then those pages must be the printouts for the A24 Usage logs! This entire time there's been a list of people who used the Andromeda 24-inch telescope. It might just be the clue we need. And I know where to look.

"Gunther," I whisper. "Follow me."

"Okay."

The two of us stay behind as the rest of the group heads up the observatory's spiral staircase. Then we re-enter the lobby and slink down the hallway into the astronomy classroom.

Once inside, I grab the file folder Ju knocked out of the rack on the night that telescope went nuts. "Bingo. The A24 usage logs." I flip through to find the page from the date in question.

I scan the paper carefully. But there are no names, only initials.

KJ. NF. LC. Ken Jennings. Noreen Feinstein. And Lin Cho.

But no AO, for Arturo Ortega.

Just as I'd theorized. My father's in the clear. He was telling the truth when he said he arrived after all the other visiting scientists. But my relief lasts only for a second.

This proves Dr. Cho is still a suspect.

Outside in the lobby a door slams. Somebody's out there whistling, and the sound is gradually getting louder. Closer.

I slide the log printouts back into the hanging folder.

Seconds later Oliver saunters into the classroom. "Hey, guys. No observatory time tonight?"

"Uh...yeah, we were just going there." I glance at Gunther, giving him the eye. *Back me up.* "But Gunther, uh, he thought he left his iPad down here."

"Yeah." He holds his iPad high in the air. "Had it in my bag the entire time. Duh!"

"Glad you didn't lose it." Oliver does a three-sixty in the center of the room. "Well, I'm going to have to lock up the classrooms for the night, now."

I nod. "Right. Of course." I wish I could spend another ten minutes with the A24 logs, but it's clear that can't happen now. Not with Oliver on patrol.

Gunther and I walk out slowly, casually. Then we sit on a bench in the lobby, start breathing normally again, and update our notes.

_ALIBI:_
Dr. Arturo Ortega was not in the country at the time of the telescope incident.

_HYPOTHESIS:_
One of the other three visiting scientists caused the telescope to move on its own: Dr. Lin Cho, Dr. Kenneth Jennings, or Dr. Noreen Feinstein.

# THROWBACK: FIFTH GRADE
# LOS TRES TURKEYS

Two years ago, on Thanksgiving afternoon, I jammed a pin into Mauna Kea on my world map, wondering if my father would be eating turkey in a few hours, in Hawaii.

"Hey." My mother stood in the doorway in her scrubs. "I'm sorry I can't go with you to dinner tonight."

I wasn't happy about Ma working today, either. I sighed, sat up on the bed and looked at her. "Yeah. Me too."

She sat next to me. "You know I wouldn't take this night shift if I didn't have to." She leaned sideways and bumped my shoulder. "Promise to bring me home a big plate of Los Tres Turkeys?"

I giggled at the name we'd given to our family's Thanksgiving tradition. Which, believe it or not, meant making three different turkeys. Great-Aunt Lala always carved out large slivers from her bird and replaced them with slow-roasted pork, making the turkey look like it had tiger stripes. Tío Marcelo deep fried his crispy masterpiece in a big stainless steel cooker out on the fire escape. But my favorite was, and still is, the turkey Tía

Sonia makes in the oven. It looks pretty standard, but it's the juiciest, best-tasting turkey in the world.

Ma patted my knee. "Maybe this time you can get your aunt to finally divulge her special ingredient?"

I smiled. Tía Sonia kept the secret recipe from everyone in the family, including Ma. "OK. I'll try."

# CHAPTER FIFTEEN:
# IN THE DARK

Javi and I enter the apartment to find Pa and Christina in the living room, sitting at opposite ends of the sofa. They look like they're waiting for a bus. Or maybe just for someone to come in and give them special instructions on how to talk to each other.

Ma is pacing in the kitchen, having an intense phone conversation. "It's not your fault, Sonia...no, no...the most important thing is that you all get better."

"Hi." I wave. "Just came from the observatory."

Ma's footfalls get louder and faster in the kitchen. "No, I can't get someone to cover last minute for Thanksgiving on such short notice."

Pa clears his throat. "I took the chance of coming here in hopes of speaking to Christina and...Javier, of course."

He looks at Javi, eyes widening, and stands. "My goodness. You're a man now."

Stoned-faced, my brother takes off his coat and hangs it in the hallway. "Yeah, well. It has been ten years since you made your way back to this town, so..."

"Yes." My father sighs. "Far too long."

Javi crosses his arms, not saying another word. But the stern look on his face says he's not in the mood to play nice with his absentee dad.

Christina looks up finally. Her eyes are red, her makeup's smeared. She eyes the doorway like she's calculating if she can make a run for it.

Ma enters the living room just then. "That was my sister. The entire family has come down with pink eye. It's three days before Thanksgiving. How's that for timing?" She rubs her forehead, looking exhausted.

"Then...they can't host us?" Christina whispers, eyes wide with horror.

Ma shakes her head. "I'm afraid not, mamita."

"But we always have Thanksgiving there. What are we going to do now?" I ask.

"I don't know." Ma throws her hands in the air. "I can't take off work either."

Pa clears his throat. "No problem. I'll have the kids over to my place for Thanksgiving."

All three of us gape at him for a moment.

I expect my mother to say, 'no' right away, but she doesn't. "Really?" Then her shoulders sag, as if she's just plain relieved. "Oh, that'd be such a big help, Arturo. I...I'll take care of dessert."

"Wait a minute." Christina stands, fists clenched. "What?"

Javi snorts. "You're kidding, right? Spend Thanksgiving with *him?*"

Ma shoots him a narrow-eyed, piercing look. "Unless you're okay with ordering pizza."

He holds up a hand. "All right, we get it, Ma."

As I slip out of my coat, I think of all the times I've wished I could spend a holiday – any holiday – with my father. Of course, it'll be strange not eating Los Tres Turkeys with Nilda and Freddie on Thanksgiving. But you can't exactly have a nice holiday meal when the host family has crusty, itchy eyes pink as a white rabbit's. So unless we want to stay home while Ma's at work, Thanksgiving with Pa makes the most sense.

"The condo apartment where we're staying has a full kitchen and a table more than large enough to fit all five of us," Pa says.

My brother frowns. "Four. Ma just said she couldn't go."

Christina chuckles bitterly. "Oh Javi, you just don't have a clue." She jumps up and rushes out of the room, sobbing.

Javi still doesn't know about Dr. Cho.

Pa takes off his glasses, folds them and sets them carefully on the side table. The he rubs the bridge of his nose. "Magda, Ignacio? Please let me have a few minutes alone with my oldest son."

Twenty minutes later, I'm up on the roof with my binoculars. The earlier clouds have vanished. The sky is clear. I stare at what's visible of the Orion Nebula.

The door to the stairwell creaks open. My father takes a few steps in my direction and then hesitates, swiveling back toward the door. Where he freezes. "Oh, my." He clears his throat. "You mind giving me a hand? It's quite dark up here."

"Sure thing." I take him by the arm and guide him to the center, the best spot to view the sky because it's the darkest. "It always takes a few minutes for my eyes to adjust. I mean...I don't have to tell you that. What a dumb thing to say."

"Not dumb at all," he says. "I left my glasses downstairs. So I appreciate the help."

"Of course." It hits me that I'm out here on the roof, alone with my father. I hold out my binoculars. "Here. Check out Orion."

He sniffs. "Oh. Uh...." He shuffles past and stares at the New York City skyline in the distance. "No thanks."

*No thanks?*

We finally have the chance, for the first time in our lives, to share the sky with each other. Why would he refuse? I leave my arm extended, like that will somehow change his mind.

He doesn't turn back. Under his breath, he says, "I shouldn't have come out here."

Is it my puny little binoculars? Not good enough for the big-shot scientist snob. "I know these can't compete with the world's best telescopes, but they're what I have."

112

"Ignacio. Do you think I'd pass judgment on your binoculars?" He sticks his hands in his coat pockets. "I helped your mother pick those out, you know."

"Oh."

I *didn't* know. Ma never told me.

"Glad to hear you've enjoyed them. I remember your mother emailing me that Christmas. Said you ran right up to the roof after opening the box." He clears his throat. "But since you're now spending your Friday nights at the observatory, I'm sure you're ready for something bigger and better to use up on this roof."

"I still love them. They're here for me anytime I have to clear my mind." I stare down at the binoculars. "I was just trying to figure out why you didn't want to be up here with – "

"I never said I didn't want to be up here." He reaches out and rests a hand on my shoulder. "It's just that...well, I thought I'd be okay up on this roof, but I...I'm not too comfortable. Mind walking me over to the stairwell?"

What's this? Is my father afraid of heights? That might explain his strange behavior. "Yeah. Sure. Here, it's over this way." I guide him back to the door.

When we open it, Cory starts barking his head off, the furry little beast.

"That dog." My father hooks his elbow in mine. "Is it...on the steps? Don't want to trip over him."

"Nah. He just likes to bark and sniff from inside the Milcus's door. He's one protective little guy."

Pa grabs the rail, and we slowly make our way down the steps, him in front, me following.

We reach the first floor and enter the kitchen. Javi and Christina are nowhere in sight, but my mother is sitting at the table, studying, textbooks piled around her.

"Don't forget these." She holds out my father's glasses.

"Oh, that's where I left them." He nods and puts them on, his hand shaking a bit. "Thank you, Magda."

He seems...nervous. I never pictured him so vulnerable. I walk him to the front door. "See you Thursday."

He tilts his head. "Thursday?"

"You know...Thanksgiving." My heart starts racing. Has he already forgotten what he's promised? "Turkey and all that."

"Of course." He smiles. "I was still distracted, from when I thought I'd lost my glasses. See you on Thursday."

# CHAPTER SIXTEEN: VOTE TODAY

After school on Monday, Ju, Gunther, and I meet in the computer lab. Mr. Orin finally convinced the school to use online ballots for the Choose Your Own Field Trip contest. The three of us each sit in front of one of the computer lab screens once the vote goes live at three o'clock. Lots of seventh graders have the same idea. Every spot in the lab is taken.

The Dolton Middle School drama club's leading man, Raj Gupta, is sharing a computer with Sara Baker, the seventh grade diva of the century. But they seem more interested in giggling and holding hands than in the voting. They've been all snuggly like that ever since last month when they starred opposite each other in the school play, *Seriousland.*

Gunther's in the chair behind me. Ju taps away on the keyboard at the station across.

My school portal profile appears onscreen with a big red checkmark icon, and the words VOTE NOW: GRADE 7 FIELD TRIP.

I click on the link.

Dolton Middle School
CHOOSE YOUR FIELD TRIP CONTEST BALLOT
Grade 7

Please rank your top three selections:
___ Barton Biosphere
___ George Washington's Headquarters
___ Jersey Devil Trail
___ Liberty Hall Museum
___ Monmouth Battle Field State Park
___ Newark Museum
___ Sterling Hill Mining Museum
___ Write in _____

"What?" I whisper and sink into my chair. No Science Slumber Party on the ballot? And no Sloan Observatory? What happened? "Ju, Gunther. Come here."

They roll their chairs over in front of my computer.

"Looks like three of us voting for the Science Slumber Party wasn't enough," I whisper.

Ju shrugs. "Guess it was kind of a long shot."

I shake my head. "I don't know why they bother asking for nominations if they don't intend to include them."

Gunther puffs out his cheeks. "At least they put in the biosphere and trail."

I'm not ready to give up on the observatory without a fight. "What if we can get more students excited so they'll write in a vote?"

"Good idea, Soto."

Ju nods. "Let's do our own write-in votes first."

We complete our online ballots just as Elijah Roberts appears in the doorway of the lab. Who better to spread enthusiasm and interest than Elijah the Excited? The three of us jump up and rush over, nearly knocking him down as he enters. He steps back just outside the computer lab again, looking nervous. "Whoa. *Sorry* guys. Didn't mean to get in your way."

"Elijah!" I try to gently grab his arm. "Before you vote. Can we talk to you about...well, a problem. This entire voting process hasn't been truly democratic, you see. And we know how strongly you feel about a fair process."

*"Yes.* Of course." He nods forcefully, head bobbing multiple times. "What's *happened?"*

"Well." Ju drapes an arm around his shoulders. "The three of us each nominated the Lenape Environmental Center Science Slumber Party for the seventh grade field trip."

*"Ooh,* I've been *there!"* His dark brown eyes light up. "My family went to the Barton Biosphere. Pretty *amazing.* I really *loved* it."

"And they've got a lot more than that to offer, Roberts." Gunther pats Elijah on the back, maybe a little too hard. "Like the Jersey Devil Trail."

I lean into him. "And an observatory where you can see star clusters, planets, and the moon's craters up close."

"Yeah, yeah." Elijah's eyebrows pop up. He bounces on the balls of his feet as if he just might flip a somersault. "I've *always* wanted to look through that *telescope,* but we always go during the *day."*

"See, that's the thing," I say. "If we do the Science Slumber Party field trip, we can do all of it. The observatory, the trail, the biosphere."

His smile widens. "Wow. Like a big *sleepover?* A whole *night?"*

"But..." Gunther shakes his head. "Big problem. They didn't even list our nomination on the ballot."

Elijah's jaw drops. "What? But that's not fair. Our voices must be heard."

"Exactly." I nod. "They can't ignore all the students if enough of us speak up. That's why we need your help to spread the word about our plan."

"Yes, pretty please." Ju clasps her hands in front of her, literally begging Elijah to join us.

He grins. "I'm in! What do you need me to do?"

We huddle in the corner to tell him how we want to gather a majority in write-in votes. Then the four of us scan the computer lab.

"All right." I cross my arms over my chest and nod. "I got the first row. Ju, you get the next one, then Gunther.

Elijah, you talk to everyone in the row closest to the door. "Now, let's do this!"

I stayed late at school to drum up support for the write-in vote, but I still make it home before Javi, who's apparently still in class. Christina is nowhere to be found, either. This is one of those days when Ma has to pull double duty. She had a morning shift at the hospital and now has class tonight. So she's probably taking a nap.

I tiptoe into the kitchen and grab some apple juice. I toss the mail I got out of our box onto the table. A grocery store circular, a couple of bills. And a postcard from my father. How strange to get one now, after all that's happened, and with him being here now. The postcard's got a picture of Big Ben on it: It's from London.

*Javier, Christina, and Ignacio,*

*My guess is you'll receive this after we've spoken in person. In London for a few days, dealing with some personal matters. No research this time.*

*See you soon, in New Jersey.*

*Cheers (as they say in England),*
*Your father*

My ears burn. Our father could've let us know he was actually on his way before he sent this last postcard.

But...no, he seems to think this is some kind of fun game for us. Figuring out cryptic messages about "personal matters," whatever that means.

My mother stands in the kitchen doorway. Her hair's matted down on one side of her head. She sighs as she enters the kitchen, still looking sleepy. "How was school?"

"Oh, hey." I tuck the postcard with the other mail. "Did I wake you up?"

"No, no. A half hour nap is my limit." She smiles, but it doesn't hide that her eyes look kind of puffy. "Haven't been sleeping too well. Not that I ever get enough rest, but it's been...more difficult these past couple of weeks."

"Since Pa came." I sit at the table. My turn to sigh.

"Well...yes."

"Last night..."I clear my throat. "Um, he mentioned that you two email each other."

She yawns. "Sometimes, after Christmas, and around your birthdays. Once the three of you stopped speaking to him, it was the easiest way for the two of us to keep in touch."

I sniff. "And he didn't email you that he was coming?"

"No," she says. "Your father isn't exactly a planner."

"Why didn't you tell us that you've been emailing him this entire time?"

She squints at me. "What's really bothering you, Ignacio?"

"Pa said you told him how I reacted back when I got the binoculars." I set down my glass harder than I'd intended. "And that he helped pick them out, and...I don't know. It seems like an important detail, you know?"

She blinks, and then stares hard at me as if she's not sure what to say. "Yes, he gave me some guidance in choosing the binoculars. He told me I should say they were from me. He wanted to pay for them. But I insisted we split the cost."

"So they were a gift from both of you?"

"Yes." She lays a hand on my arm. "He didn't want you to refuse a gift from him, like Christina and Javi had done. And you do love those binoculars, Ig."

"Yeah." I nod. "I do." I don't think anyone – not Ma, Pa, even Ju – knows what these binoculars mean to me. I can't imagine my life without this connection to the sky.

# CHAPTER SEVENTEEN: THANKSGIVING

J avi, Christina, and I walk down the hallway of the building where Pa and Dr. Cho are being housed. Each of us is carrying a different homemade dessert.

Ma had yesterday off, so she blasted her favorite old-time salsa music while she baked three different recipes: pumpkin pie, flan, and cookies.

The pumpkin pie, still warm in my hands, smells like cinnamon and pumpkin and nutmeg. "You think they'll mind if we start with dessert?" I ask.

"Turkey's the whole point. And the stuffing. And the mashed potatoes." Javi licks his lips as he balances the big tray of butter cookies. "Man, I'm hungry. I'm gonna miss having Los Tres Turkeys this year."

The last door on the right flies open and a Bing Crosby holiday recording plays.

*I'll be home for Christmas.*
*You can count on me.*

For a second, I wonder if Pa timed opening the door at that exact moment as his way of saying he'll be here in New Jersey until Christmas.

"Happy Turkey Day!" Pa springs out, wrapped in a big white chef's apron.

No, the song isn't a secret message. It just happens to be playing. He's probably streaming a Christmas station on his computer. Besides, Dolton's not home to him.

Shuffling their feet, looking down at their desserts, Christina and Javi each mumble hello.

"Hi. I...uh..." Unsure of what else to say, I hold out the pie dish. "I've got pumpkin pie."

"Smells delectable." Pa smiles and waves a hand. "Come in! Come in!"

We file inside like we're lining up for an assembly in the auditorium at school. Me. Javi. Christina. The three of us stand awkwardly in the wide foyer, looking around at the condo. There aren't any walls between the kitchen, the dining table, and the living room. A row of tall windows in the back let in the low afternoon sun. The furniture is beige leather and light wood. The walls are all white. Ma would call this color scheme boring. Nothing like her colorful childhood home in Cuba. But it's fine for a rented condo where Pa and Dr. Cho are staying for a few weeks.

The table in the dining area has a decorative vinyl tablecloth printed with autumn leaves. There's a line of prepared dishes sitting along the kitchen island counter. Dr. Cho sets a basket of dinner rolls on the table and rushes over to hug me. "Good to see you again, Ignacio." She takes the pumpkin pie and adds it to the buffet set up.

"Um, yeah. Happy Thanksgiving."

She turns to Javi and Christina. "I'm Lin. Artie's told me so much about you both." She takes the cookies from my brother and sets them on the counter, next to a basket filled with potpourri. "It's so nice to meet you at last."

"Um...watch the flan juice, Chris," I say. A patch of sweet brown caramel has leaked onto the sleeve of my sister's coat.

Christina twists her arm to see where the coat's been stained. "Oh, man. I just got this."

"No problem. Take the coat right off. We'll have that sleeve as good as new by the time you leave." Dr. Cho reaches for the flan.

Christina hands over the dripping platter. "Oh. Um, OK. Thanks," she mumbles and then slides out of her lavender ski jacket.

Dr. Cho rushes the flan to the kitchen counter like it's been prepped for emergency surgery.

"Laundry facilities are just down the hall." Pa grabs the jacket and rushes out the still-open front door. It feels sort of like we're on a Netflix medical drama.

Javi and I go over and hang our coats on a wooden rack by the door. He wanders into the living room and snatches up a piece of salami and cheese from a big platter on the

124

coffee table in front of the leather sofa. "Mmm. That's good cheese."

Dr. Cho is still at the counter, trying to soak up the brown sugary liquid still leaking from the sides of the flan, by sticking bunches of paper towels around the plate.

"Ma should've used larger dishes," Christina says, like she's some kind of baking expert. "See, now you've got to flip it onto another plate. There's a specific way to do it. I mean, sorry, but... you probably wouldn't know how."

Dr. Cho flaps a hand at Christina, as if to say that, on the contrary, she is in fact a master of the Flan Universe. "Oh, I know all about flipping flans. When we visited Cuba I watched Pito, Artie's cousin – and well, your cousin, too. Anyway, he flipped several flans during our visit."

Christina raises her eyebrows. "Cuba, huh?" She looks at Javi and me as if to ask, *Why does she get to meet our family?*

And I have to agree. "Really? We've never been to Cuba." Nothing against Dr. Cho, but somehow it seems unfair that she's met Pa's family in Cuba and we haven't, not ever.

Javi stacks four pieces of cheese on a single cracker. "So what's it like?"

She gazes past us dreamily, as if the memory's painted in tropical colors on the white condo wall. "Charming and sad all at once. Colorful, lively. Can't beat the weather, of course. Pito lives only a few blocks away from the ocean, by a beach that was simply pristine. And I swear, half the town was related to Artie. More cousins than I could count."

125

I imagine me, Christina, and Javi strolling down a narrow street like the one in the painting above the sofa in our living room. And people shouting from car windows and porches – *Mira, los ninos de Arturo!* Arturo's kids. Family always recognizes family, right? But in my mind, our faces are featureless, just like the eerie artwork above the sofa in our living room. My heart sinks. Would our Cuban cousins even recognize us if we did go there?

"What's Pito like?" I ask, mostly to get the sadness out of my head.

"He can catch fish quicker than anyone I've ever met." Dr. Cho picks up her phone, tapping a few times. She holds her phone's screen out to show us a tall, thin man with a dark complexion winking at the camera, holding up a big silver fish on a line. He's probably a little younger than Pa. She swipes and shows us another picture. This one of about twenty people of all ages posing in front of a tall palm tree. The ocean sparkles in the background. My father and Dr. Cho both have their arms around people who are also our family. Yet I recognize none of them. "This was your great-uncle's birthday celebration," she says.

"They sure seem to like Pa," Javi says.

Dr. Cho smiles. "Are you kidding? He's a celebrity. Pride and joy of the whole town. You'll have to go down there with him someday."

Javi steps back. "Oh, yeah. He's mentioned so often how he wants to take us to a whole bunch of places. You know. Someday."

126

"Yeah." I yank at the sleeve of my brown sweater. "Just not today."

Dr. Cho laughs. "He does say that a lot."

We don't laugh with her.

Christina crosses her arms. "But you've been to all of those same places with him."

She clears her throat. "Oh. Well...just some."

"I'll bet." Christina chuckles.

What Dr. Cho's saying, it doesn't seem fair.

Christina picks up a tiny pinecone from a basket of potpourri and sniffs it. "Ugh. I hate fake apple cinnamon."

Dr. Cho eyes the pinecone. "I'm happy to move it into another room if you'd like."

"Never mind. It's not that serious." My sister tosses the pinecone back on top of the flower petals and stems. "I'll deal. We're all used to dealing."

"No, it's not a problem. I want you to feel comfortable." Dr. Cho picks up the basket of potpourri, her hand slightly shaking.

My father suddenly steps through the apartment door, singing "Walking in a Winter Wonderland." Dr. Cho flinches and drops the basket. Apple cinnamon potpourri explodes across the pale carpet.

"Oh, honey." He holds up both hands. "Sorry! Didn't mean to scare you."

"No, no, I was just, um, putting this in another room." She looks flustered as she kneels to pick up the scattered bits of potpourri.

All of us, even Christina, get down then and help clean the mess, though in complete silence. But after a few moments my stomach growls so loud, it sounds like a ravenous panther is about to escape from inside me.

Javi stands and pats his belly. "We're all kind of hungry, as you can hear."

"Um, *hello,*" Christina says. "That was *my* stomach."

"No. It was mine," Pa and I say in unison.

Dr. Cho sits back, laughing.

"What's so funny, honey?"

"I could've sworn it was mine." She grabs her belly, really cracking up.

Then it happens again. Someone else's stomach growls like a wild animal, and we all burst into laughter. Forgetting the anger and awkwardness that has filled the room since we arrived.

It really is time to celebrate Thanksgiving.

# CHAPTER EIGHTEEN:
# BRIGHTNESS

The whole stomach-growling thing lifted everyone's mood. By early evening the sun has set, but the lighting in the condo is bright and cheerful as we sit at the long table enjoying the delicious meal.

I cover a turkey drumstick with mashed potatoes and pour gravy over the entire thing. I slice some off and take a bite. The gravy's the perfect amount of salty. The potatoes so creamy and buttery.

"I must say, Christina. It's quite impressive that your blog has an international readership already," Dr. Cho says.

Pa nods. "Means you know how to connect with people. That's a great, useful skill."

"Please." Javi snorts. "I could start a YouTube channel with videos of the neighbor's hyper Yorkie. I'd be a viral sensation."

My father clicks his tongue. "Now, Javier."

"Just joking." My brother rolls his eyes. "Geez."

"What are your plans for after college, Javier?" Pa asks.

"I'll spend a year or two working full-time at the metal shop in the next town over," he says. "Then I want to start my own business. Reclaimed materials. That's my thing."

"No kidding." Pa sits back in the chair and smiles as if pleasantly surprised. "Excellent idea."

I finish my drumstick while Pa asks Javi all about metalwork for several minutes.

Dr. Cho turns to me. "What about you, Ignacio? Anything exciting going on at school?"

"Yeah." I swallow the last bite of food, washing it down with a gulp of ginger ale. "We have this contest to pick the location of our next field trip."

I explain how we organized the write-in votes for the Science Slumber Party.

"A fun choice." Dr. Cho nods and takes a sip of wine. "The center has so many excellent educational programs."

"The school has never done an overnight field trip before, though," I tell her. "Between me and my friends, I think we got around fifty votes. Hope that's enough."

"Good to hear you're taking initiative with this contest." Pa tosses his napkin on his plate. "It takes effort to make something happen."

Effort. Like the way our father is just now making such an effort to learn about who we are, when he should already know this stuff. Was effort what was missing all these years? Is that what kept him from coming to see us in Dolton...not enough effort?

My fingers tingle so hard, I drop my fork. It clangs against the plate.

"What's wrong, Ig?" Christina frowns at me.

"Uh, nothing." But I can feel my face twisting, tensing up all over.

Javi looks around at the half-full platters and containers spread across the table. "Sure is a lot of leftovers."

"Well, you guys are taking most of it home." Pa holds up a hand to stop us from arguing over this fact. "Leftovers for tomorrow. And definitely, a nice, big plate for your mother to enjoy when she gets home from her shift at the hospital."

"I'll make it." I look him right in the eye. "I know what she likes. Like crispy turkey skin."

Pa laughs. "That's right. I'd forgotten."

I'll bet he did. What else has he forgotten? I want to shove back my chair, stand up and yell, *Why don't you know us? Why don't you know me!*

All those interviews and articles I've read about him and posted on my wall. My map that tracks everywhere he's been. I always thought knowing where he was would help me know him better. But knowing his location, or what he's researching – that's not really knowing him.

"Yo, Ig." Javi snaps his fingers in front of my face. "I asked you a question."

"Sorry. Must've zoned out."

He shakes his head. "I said, won't you be creeped out spending the night at that center since it's up on a mountain in the middle of nowhere?"

I shrug. "No. It's peaceful."

"The environmental center's as secure as they come." Dr. Cho dabs the corners of her mouth with her napkin. "Cameras everywhere."

"Oh good," Javi says. "So when midnight hits and the Jersey Devil jumps out of a tree and eats ya'll up, there'll be video evidence for the cops to pursue the case."

Pa laughs. "No doubt. Apparently, they even have a video of me walking into a storage closet that I thought was the conference room."

Dr. Cho rubs his arm. "Well, honey, those doors are easily confused, even for people who aren't – "

My father sighs and abruptly takes off his glasses. "Lin...I'm not sure this is the right time."

"Oh, Artie." Dr. Cho tilts her head. "Then, when? These are your kids."

"What's going on?" Javi crosses his arms and frowns at both of them.

Christina shakes her head. "I don't get it. Why did the two doors confuse you? "

My ears burn. "And why does she get to know your big secret, and meet our family in Cuba, and travel around the world with you?" I can't control it anymore. Can't hold it in. I'm tired of being left out. I don't care how nice Dr. Cho is. That doesn't make up for, well,  anything. "We're your kids. Your family. She isn't."

"Ignacio." My father's face looks stern, and disappointed.

My throat tightens. I have to get out of here. It's too bright. Too many people. I need space. To be alone.

I burst out of the condo, rushing outside into air so cold it freezes the breath in my lungs. What was I thinking coming out here without a coat? But I can't go back there. Not until I can slow my racing heart. Not until I can control my runaway mouth. Christina and Javi are the ones who talk back sometimes. I never do. I never have. Until now.

I dash around to the side of the condo where there are no street lamps in sight. The trees there block out the New York City skyline, and the moon above them is new. I look east. There's Betelgeuse, the red supergiant that will explode into an impossibly bright supernova sometime in the next million years.

That's how I felt inside the condo. Like I was about to go supernova and burst. Out here, at least I can breathe.

Light footsteps rush along the walkway behind me, and then crunch across the frozen brown grass. "You must be freezing, Ignacio." Dr. Cho few stands a feet away, holding out my coat.

Hot as my ears are, the rest of me *is* freezing. "Um, great. Thanks." I grab the coat and put it on. "How'd you know I was back here?"

She glances up. "Figured you'd find the darkest spot in the complex. A place where you could look up and spot some stars."

"Did you and Pa tell Javi and Christina his big secret?"

"It isn't mine to tell." She lets out a long breath, like a slow sigh. "Artie's telling your brother and sister right now. He wants to talk to you, too. When you're ready."

I stare back up at Betelgeuse. "I don't like it when you call him Artie."

She doesn't say anything to that. Not right away. "I'm not your enemy, Ignacio. I'm not trying to be your mother, either. And you should know that your father...that he loves you. Very much. Even if he hasn't been...."

"Around much? A regular father? The kind who pushes his kids on a swing, signs up to be the class parent on a field trip? The kind of dad who shows up on your birthday when he promised to." I sniff back tears. "All I've got of him are some podcasts, a few television shows, and a stack of postcards."

"I won't pretend to know all that's happened between you three and him." Dr. Cho says. She's silent for a moment. "But I've seen him when he's choosing a postcard for you. Usually, he'll buy a bunch, and then deliberate for an hour or more over which is the perfect one to send. Which landscape would be most wonderful to show you himself, someday. He's constantly talking about taking all three of you on a global adventure, once you're done with high school."

Graduation from high school? That seems like a lifetime away. And he never told us any of this. I feel a sinking deep in my stomach. "So...we have to wait five years to see him again?"

"No. Not at all. What I meant, is... She shakes her head. "He wants to spend at least a few weeks traveling with

134

you, but he wants to respect your mother's wishes, too. For stability, and all that. So it has to happen after high school. But he's also mentioned visiting Dolton more often. Especially since this facility is being equipped now with – "

A cold wind blows, we both shiver. "With what?" I ask.

Another frigid gust. I pull the collar of my coat up to my ears.

"Why don't we head inside so your father can tell you himself?" Dr. Cho asks.

I take another look at Betelgeuse, that brilliant supergiant star with a mass so great it tugs at everything around it with its tremendous gravity. Kind of like my father. But when I look at all of Orion, Betelgeuse is only a small part of that constellation. And I guess that's like my father too.

"Okay." I nod. "Let's go back in."

# CHAPTER NINETEEN: LEFTOVERS

Back inside the condo, Javi, Christina, and Dr. Cho get the dessert ready. My father and I sit across the table from each other, almost like we're in a meeting. He looks a little nervous, but also kind of sad.

"So, you see..." He pauses and exhales. "My sight began rapidly deteriorating several months ago."

Oh, I think. So that's it.

Because certain things now make sense, when I think back. Like my father's strange behavior on the roof last week, when I had to almost lead him to the door and down the stairs. And his being driven around by a car service.

*Visual impairment.* But...but...he's an astrophysicist. Everything he does involves looking, seeing at night.

"Do they know what caused it?" I ask.

"I've been to several specialists. All agree this condition was likely the result of some bug I picked up in my travels. In fact, I had a follow-up appointment with a specialist in London before coming here. That's why I arrived a few days after Lin. Did you get my postcard from London?"

I nod. "Just a little while ago. Can you still...see the sky?"

"Certain things, depending on the kind of equipment in a facility." Pa takes off his glasses. "But my vision will continue to get worse, I'm afraid."

"Are you going to have to stop working?" I stare at the Thanksgiving tablecloth. "I mean, like, switch to another job?" I can't even begin to imagine that: My father, without the stars.

He pauses, then shakes his head. "I hope not. There's been some amazing progress with accessibility in observing the cosmos. Perhaps you're familiar with Wanda Diaz Merced and her work on the sonification of data?"

I shake my head. "You mean, like, seeing it with sound?"

He smiles. "Exactly. Dr. Diaz Merced is the blind astrophysicist who created the field of sonic astronomy. She takes the visual data, and converts it into sound so she can analyze it by ear."

"Hey. That's pretty cool." I smile.

"In fact, the reason Lin and I are here at the Lenape Environmental Center is to evaluate the accessibility of

137

the facilities. We'll be making recommendations on ways to make sure people with impairments get a full experience during their visit."

Dr. Cho walks over and lays a hand on his shoulder. Pa reaches up to squeeze it. Even with what sounds to me like very be bad news, right now Pa seems happy. It feels so strange to think it, but I can see that Dr. Cho makes sense for him. She *gets* him, in a way Ma never really could. It feels like I'm betraying my mother just by having these thoughts, though.

Christina sets down the glistening flan Ma baked. I can smell the sweet caramel from here. I look over at the pumpkin pie, and cookies already sitting on the table. No Los Tres Turkeys, but still ... three desserts. And suddenly it's like, in a way, Ma's here, too.

"Ma's the best baker in the world," Javi says. "Isn't she?"

I nod. "Oh, yeah. In fact, the best in this galaxy."

On the ride home the streets are eerily still and quiet, like the snow is a blanket they're all tucked under to sleep.

"I didn't know what to expect tonight." Christina is riding in the passenger seat with a huge shopping bag of leftovers on her lap. "Pa, going blind? I didn't see that coming. What I don't get, though, is why he hasn't just told people. I mean, sure-some might look at him differently. But it's nothing to be ashamed of."

Javi shrugs. "His life will change a lot once everyone knows."

I nod. "Maybe he wants to choose when that happens."

We're stopped at a light, waiting to turn onto Main Street. Javi makes the turn, and soon we're approaching the public library. A guy is skateboarding down the steps, leaving long lines of tracks in the snow. Green army coat. Long blond hair. Ponytail. The same one from the gazebo. The same guy my father and I saw during the car ride that night he arrived in town.

"Hey, that's Jack Lenihan," Christina says with concern in her voice. "Pull over."

Javi slowly pulls to the curb.

Christina rolls down her window, letting cold air and light snowflakes inside. "Jack!"

The guy must not hear her. He runs back up the library steps and rides along the dark, awning-covered stoop. Leaps over the staircase and lands at the bottom. Rolling out, he collapses and lands on his back. He doesn't move for a few seconds.

"Oh, no!" Christina cries. She jumps out of the car, carrying one of the containers of leftovers, and slams the door behind her.

"You think he's hurt?" I ask Javi.

"Hope not." He peers out the window at the fallen skater.

Christina approaches Jack. I see her mouth open, though her voice is too muffled through the window to make out the words.

Jack sits up quickly like he's surprised to see someone else there. Then he stands and brushes snow from his coat. The two of them talk for a couple of minutes. He does a lot of shrugging. He takes the food when Christina holds

139

the container out to him. Under the yellow light of the street lamps, my sister is the very picture of holiday spirit.

Jack trudges up to the library steps with the leftovers in one hand, the skateboard under his other arm. He waves back at us.

Christina shouts, "Happy Thanksgiving!" before getting back into the car. She shivers as she pulls the door shut. "Brrr, that cold's no joke. Can't imagine being outside in it for hours."

"Seriously. He's going to stay out here?" Javi asks.

She stares out the window. "I asked if he wanted to come over, but he said he'll just eat on the steps."

Javi shakes his head. "Pretty dark and cold out there."

"What about his family?" I ask. "I mean, it's Thanksgiving."

"Holidays are hard for some people." She stares out the window, but doesn't say anything else.

Javi shifts the car into drive. "That was nice of you." Snow swirls ahead of the car as he pulls back onto the road. "For real."

"Yeah," I agree.

She takes a long time adjusting the heating vents. "I just hope things get better for him."

Our family is far from perfect, but I can't imagine things ever getting so bad that I'd rather hang outside in the snow than be with them on Thanksgiving.

I lean forward to say over the front seat, "Makes you think – as much drama as we've had with Pa, I guess we still had a good Thanksgiving."

# CHAPTER TWENTY:
# AUDIBLE SPACE

The day after Thanksgiving, Ju, Gunther, and I are the only ones who turn up at the observatory for Cosmic Night. We've got a few minutes before Kamir will lead us into the dome.

I wave my friends over to the back of the gas giants exhibit. "I've got to tell you both something that's not related to the case. At least, I don't think it is."

"Everything okay, Soto?" Gunther whispers, looking concerned.

Ju leans toward me. "What is it, Ig?"

I take a deep breath. "My father's losing his vision."

My friends are silent for a moment. I guess they're shocked by the news, too.

Ju's eyes widen with concern. "How? What damaged his eyesight?"

"He said they think it happened because of a virus he caught."

"Wow." Gunther frowns. "That's intense. Got to be tough for him. I mean, like, isn't space all about what stuff scientists can see out there?"

"Yeah, but you can also observe by listening," I say. "That's what visually impaired people do in everyday life."

"Listening to space?" Ju tilts her head, confused. "I don't get it."

"Basically, he'll take data that the telescopes gather and convert it into audio files. And get this, Ju. The scientist who came up with the idea? Her name is Dr. Wanda Diaz Merced. She's from Puerto Rico."

"Cool!" She smiles. "Boricua in space!"

I laugh. "More like a Boricua *observing* space. And because of the work she's done, my father can keep on studying the cosmos."

"What's her name again?" Gunther opens his iPad. "I want to hear this for myself."

"Look up 'Wanda Diaz Merced' and 'sonic files,' " I tell him.

He types the words in and then starts scrolling. "Audio file of a gamma-ray burst?"

I nod. "That's her. Play it!"

Gunther taps the screen, and the iPad plays a series of quick audio pulses, the pitch going high and low randomly. It's sort of like the sound of a little kid tinkering on a xylophone. But this is space, not just in images but

142

talking to us. Right there in the Lenape Environmental Center, the three of us listen to sounds representing the farthest reaches of our universe.

Ten minutes later, we're inside the observatory. The air from the open dome is so cold, even Kamir has switched out his leather jacket for a heavy-duty ski coat. He's at the computer, typing. "First up tonight is Ceres."

The telescope aligns according to the command, and the dome shifts. Kamir positions the portable metal stairs and then leans forward to look through the eyepiece. "Hm, not quite aligned." He glances at the computer screen from up on the ladder. "Hey Ig, can you please read the pop-up window on the screen?"

"Sure." I read the words aloud. "'Give a command to continue with voice recognition application.'"

*Voice recognition.* Of course. That's what my father must use when he's up here.

Kamir hops off the metal step stool and stands in front of the computer. "Exact alignment. Ceres. Go."

The telescope whirs as it shifts. I think back to how it acted on the day it went rogue. Could that have been because it was in voice recognition mode? What if, that night, we accidentally gave it a command? One that was unintentional.

"Hey, wait a minute." Gunther leans in toward the desk. "That same red light just blinked!"

Kamir climbs down. "Yeah, it does that in Accessible mode."

Ju steps up to the computer and points at the light. "I get it. ACCESS is short for accessible!"

"Hey, Kamir," I say. "The telescope has been in voice recognition mode more often than usual lately, right?"

"Yeah." Kamir nods. "Dr. Cho has been installing additional equipment into the system so that even more people can use our facilities. Soon we'll be the most accessible optical astronomical observatory in the region."

"What if the telescope didn't move on its own? What if it's been activated by what the computer thought it recognized as speech commands from some people here in the observatory?"

"Pretty good observation. Dr. Nolan and I actually figured that out a couple days ago." Kamir climbs down the portable step stool. "But how'd you kids put that all together?"

Gunther shrugs a little, as if too modest to go all out. "It's what we do."

"Yep. That's right. We're real sleuths," Ju says matter of factly.

"The Seventh Grade Sleuths, to be exact," I say.

"Well, that explains it." Kamir laughs. "Oliver said you two boys were hanging around the astronomy classroom and looking through files. Of course, I vouched for you all. Said you were just curious. Like, regular scholars of space. Didn't know you were detectives, too. Nice work, solving the mystery. But no more snooping around, though, okay? If you've got a question, just come to Dr. Nolan or me. Got it?"

"We think of a lot of questions," I warn. "You don't really know what you're asking for."

Ju and Gunther laugh.

Even Kamir joins in. "That's OK. I'll take my chances. And now..." He taps the step stool with the toe of his boot. "Who wants to go first? Ceres is ready for its close up."

When we're back in the minivan, I flick on the overhead light and yank off my gloves.

Javi shakes his head from the driver's seat. "What did I tell you about that light?"

"Hold on just a second. It won't take long," I say. "We've just got to officially close The Case of the Out of Control Telescope."

We note our final observations, as the best old detectives always have done. Gunther uncovers his iPad and taps away while Ju scribbles in her purple casebook.

I open my own casebook, too. "Our second case is officially closed."

## DATA:

*The center's telescope is connected to a voice recognition program. K. Fitzgerald confirmed that the computer was left in ACCESSIBLE mode following research sessions conducted by L. Cho.*

## ANALYSIS & RESULT:

145

We have come to the unanimous conclusion that the telescope inside the Sloan Observatory has not been hacked or tampered with. The computer used to move the telescope interpreted the casual speech of guests in the observatory as formal voice recognition commands to move the dome. This has been confirmed by K. Fitzgerald. The mysterious Case of the Out of Control Telescope has been SOLVED!

# CHAPTER TWENTY-ONE:
# CONTEST RESULTS

It's been a couple of days since we solved the case at the observatory. This morning is when we're supposed to hear the winning field trip announcement.

"Hey, Gunther! Ig!" Elijah's eyes are wide, and he's bouncing in his chair in even more excitement than usual. "You guys *ready* for the *contest results?*"

Gunther nods. "Sure. Crossing our fingers and all that."

"Yeah, man," I say. "Thanks for your help getting the word out about the write-in votes."

"You bet." Elijah grins. "I think we've got a real *shot.*"

I hope so. I can already imagine Elijah's reaction to finally looking up at Jupiter. *Wow!* This is *amazing!* Look at *all those moons!*

The bells rings and Mr. Orin stands to take attendance.

The first few announcements seem to last an hour. But finally the sixth-grader speaking on the intercom gets to the really big news. *"Every year the seventh grade votes on the Choose Your Field Trip contest. This year included lots of familiar nominations along with some exciting new ideas. The voting was tabulated by Vice Principal Belzer, PTA President Antoinette Esposito, and the student representative, eighth-grader Franklin Diaz. The panel has requested additional time to consider the options, so we will postpone naming a site at this time."*

There's a surprised and disappointed murmuring throughout the classroom. "Has this ever happened before?" "Can they even do that?" "Maybe there was a tie?"

Elijah turns back to face me and Gunther, looking deflated. He's no longer bouncing. "Guess you'll have to keep your fingers crossed a little longer."

I catch Gunther's eye. "You think this is because of our write-in votes?"

"Could be, Soto. And I know how we can find out."

I nod. "Right. Franklin Diaz."

Between first and second period, Gunther, Elijah, and I meet Ju in the hallway. Turns out she had the same idea about asking Franklin what was up. We all rush down the hall, headed for his locker.

"Diaz!" Gunther grins and zooms up to Franklin, with me, Elijah, and Ju close behind. "We heard you're student rep for the seventh grade Choose Your Field Trip Contest."

"Uh...yeah." Franklin nods, looking at us with a little trepidation. "So?"

"Wow!" Elijah's eyebrows pop up like he's just heard he won a million dollars. Suddenly he's back in bouncing form. "Maybe *I* can *volunteer* to be a judge next year."

Franklin hoists the straps of his book bag up. "Look, I don't want to be late to class, so – "

"Right." Gunther drapes an arm around his shoulders. "Real quick. What's the word on the field trip contest? Why the big delay?"

Franklin sighs. "Things got a little complicated because of a bunch of write-in votes."

Ju taps her foot. "Complicated. But how?"

"Yeah," I add. "I mean, did the write-ins win or not?"

Franklin narrows his eyes. "Why? Were you guys behind the Science Slumber Party idea?"

"Come on, Diaz, spill," Gunther says, shaking Franklin back and forth a little. But in a friendly way.

Franklin takes a deep breath. "Yes, the write-ins did get the most votes."

Elijah throws two fists high in the air. "Yes! The people have spoken."

Franklin holds up a hand. "Not so fast. We're trying to decide if those votes should be disqualified."

"But...but..." I turn up my palms in surprise. "Why even let us vote if you're not going to go with what the students want? It isn't really our choice then."

"Yeah!" Elijah's eyes are so wide now they look like they could actually pop out of his head. "Where's the *democracy* in this?"

Franklin looks up and down the hallway that's quickly emptying out, then pulls us in closer. He lowers his voice to a whisper. "They were concerned about getting all the parents to agree to an overnight trip. But if you can prove enough parents would be okay with it, they might change their minds."

"Maybe we can go around town with a door-to-door petition," Ju says.

"I don't know if there's time for all that." Franklin crosses his arms. "They want to make the final decision by Sunday night, so they can announce it next Monday morning."

"Only a week." Gunther shakes his head. "Is that even enough time to ask around?"

The warning bell sounds.

"Gotta go." Franklin rushes away, down the hall.

"I think we can do it." I grab my friends' arms. "We'll use the school's online community portal. All students and parents have access. We'll create and send out an online petition, just like Mr. Orin taught us. We can set it up in the lab after school today and make the deadline for signatures Friday night. Then email them all to Franklin on the weekend in time for the final decision!"

"Good plan, Soto." Gunther grins.

Ju nods. "Let's meet after school in the media center."

Dear Parents:

We hope you'll consider signing this petition to support a proposed seventh grade field trip to the Lenape Environmental Center, home to the Barton

Biosphere, the Jersey Devil Trail, and the Sloan Astronomical Observatory.

The trip would be a unique educational experience for students, who would learn about many areas of science at once: biology, botany, earth science, and astronomy.

We proposed the center's Science Slumber Party field trip so we and our fellow  students can experience all the center has to offer. If you agree this would be a beneficial field trip for your child, please add your name below. You can also sign up to be a chaperone.

For more information visit:
www.LenapeEC.com/Science-Slumber-Party
Thank you for considering our idea!
Sincerely,
Gunther Corrie, Justina Feliciano, and Ignacio Soto


Sunday morning, I trudge into the kitchen, following the scent of coffee and fried eggs. Christina and Javi are seated at the kitchen table, eating omelets and drinking coffee.

Ma steps away from the stove to kiss me. "Ready for a celebratory breakfast?"

I yawn. "What're we celebrating?"

Christina lifts a mug and raises it in my direction. "The *Dolton Daily* posted an article about your educational activism." She slides her phone across the table. "I reblogged it on my site."

I pick it up and read the headline.

# Seventh Grade Students Start a Movement with Successful Online Petition

The article is short, but it mentions Ju, Gunther, Elijah, and me. It even quotes the petition we sent to parents through the school online portal. The best part? It says the overnight field trip was approved and a date in April will be announced soon.

"Wow! I wasn't expecting to find out the results until tomorrow morning." I slam both palms against the tabletop. "I get to spend a whole night at the center!"

Ma adjusts the flame on the stovetop coffeemaker. "I'm happy I signed that online petition. It was much easier than I thought it'd be."

Christina leans toward me. "That's a legit achievement, Ig. When I was in seventh grade, the selection committee just gave us a list of places they'd come up with, and we had to vote on that. No write-ins or nomination round for us."

"I wonder if Ju knows. I should call her!" I jump out of my chair and grab the cordless phone from its wall mount. Before I can punch in her number the phone rings, vibrating my hand. The caller ID says FELICIANO.

"Ha! It's her." I push TALK. "Can you believe it? The Science Slumber Party is going to happen, because of us."

"We did it!" Ju squeals. "I cannot wait until April."

"That's when Jupiter and its moons will be visible," I say. "And the entire seventh grade will be there to see it."

# CHAPTER TWENTY-TWO:
# SENSORY OVERLOAD

I t's after dinner, and I'm up on the roof. Though I'm bundled up as much as possible, the icy wind still sends chills through my entire body. But the sky is cloudless tonight. Venus is clearly visible in the southwest even without my binoculars.

The door to the roof opens. I assume it's Javi, coming up to clear his mind like he sometimes does.

Instead, it's Ma in her long black winter coat. "I can't remember the last time I came up here." She shuffles over to me carefully in the dark. "I just got off the phone with your aunt. They're having an early Christmas party next Saturday with Los Tres Turkeys."

*"Yes!"* The meal with Pa and Lin was tasty, but nothing can compete with Los Tres Turkeys.

"The best part?" she adds. "I have that night off."

"Really?" I smile. "Kind of makes up for the lost Thanksgiving."

She nods. "Yeah. I hate to miss any holiday with you three."

"But you're always there whenever you can be." The truth is she's kind of been our mom *and* our dad. Dependable as the sun and moon.

"It means so much to hear that." She puts both arms around me. "What are you looking at tonight?"

"Venus."

"Oh yeah?"

"Here. Take a look." I hand her the binoculars. "It's that bright spot next to the moon."

She lifts them to her face and aims them up. "Ay, it sure does glow. Crazy to think how that tiny flash of light is practically the size of earth, only it's millions of miles away."

"One hundred sixty-two million miles. Two hundred sixty-two million kilometers."

"You're so much like your father." She lowers the binoculars. Even in the dark, I can see her eyes are watery, but she's smiling. "And that's amazing, m'ijo. Because there are so many good things about him. You got the best parts. Curiosity, sense of adventure, your great love of the stars. Heartbreaking to think he won't be able to see them anymore, soon."

"I know. But he'll still be able to listen."

She's silent for a moment. Finally, she says, "He's already started to, hasn't he?"

I nod and then look up at the sky. "Yeah."

A few days later, I follow Christina, Javi, and Ma up the three flights to my aunt's third-floor apartment. The floor vibrates with the beats of DJ Woke, also known as our cousin Freddie. I feel the steady rhythm vibrating each step.

As we approach the apartment door, Tía Sonia flings it open. Suddenly it's sensory overload – the music, the rich scent of roasting turkey, my aunt in her neon yellow apron, waving us inside, crying, "Look at all of you!" My aunt storms into the hallway and showers us with hugs and kisses. "Ready for Los Tres Turkeys?"

"I can't wait!" Javi says, as he steps into the apartment.

"Madga! Ignacio! Javier!" Several family members rush up to greet us as we all enter my aunt and uncle's apartment. It's decked out in red bows with a large nativity set next to a towering Christmas tree. The tiny family room is packed.

Great-Aunt Lala hugs and kisses the four of us. "Pero, give me those coats already." She grabs our coats and jackets, then disappears into the back of the apartment, probably to pile them on one of the beds with everyone else's.

Our little cousin Juanita runs over to Javi. "Pretend you're a monster! Pretend you're a monster!"

He raises his hands into fake claws and chases after her. "Mwahahaha!"

I wave to my cousin Freddie, who's standing behind his makeshift deejay table wearing a Miami Dolphins baseball cap turned slightly off center. "All right, all right! DJ Woke is here to make your night go right." He plays a Marc Anthony salsa song, and the music summons Tía Sonia, who dances out of the kitchen.

My cousin Nilda boogies up to me holding Desi Arnaz, a pug who's never met a face he doesn't like to lick. "Give Cousin Ig kisses, Desi," she coos.

"Hey, Nil." I lean over and laugh as the dog licks my chin. "Hey, you stinky beast." I scratch Desi Arnaz between the ears as he wriggles to escape.

"Come on, Nil!" Christina grabs my cousin's hand and pulls her into the circle of dancing women.

I sneak a peek into the kitchen where Tío Marcelo is slicing the deep-fried turkey. Juanita runs by, followed by Javi, pretending to be Frankenstein. Sure, our family can be a bit strange, but I love the holidays at my aunt and uncle's place.

"Bueno, Freddie." Tío Marcelo stands in the doorway to the kitchen. "Let's take a break from the music."

Desi Arnaz jumps to the floor, wagging his whole body as if he knows what's coming.

"Let's eat!" Tía Sonia claps her hands above her head. "A comer."

Nilda tosses her braids over her shoulders and looks over at me. And then we say what we usually say on Thanksgiving.

"What time is it?" Freddie shouts.

Nilda and I call out in unison, "Time for Los Tres Turkeys!"

My father's car service is waiting in front of the house when we get home at midnight. Ma pulls the van into our driveway, but Pa's nowhere in sight. Ma, Javi, and Christina don't seem too surprised, which I find strange. Especially since it's so late.

"Ignacio," Ma says softly. "Why don't you go on up to the roof?"

"Um...okay." There's something weird going on here. But since it's a clear night, I duck inside, grab my binoculars and take the back steps two at a time. I push hard against the heavy metal door and step out onto the rooftop.

"Hello, Ignacio," my father's voice calls to me from somewhere in the dark.

I jump. "Whoa. What're you doing up here? How'd you even..."

"I arranged it all with your mother."

"I helped him climb the steps." Dr. Lin Cho's there too, turned slightly away. All I can see is her silhouette.

"Now that you're here, I'll leave you two alone." She pats my arm and then shuts the roof door behind her, leaving my father and me alone.

"Lin helped set it up...actually, she pretty much deserves full credit." He steps aside so I can see. Even in the darkness, there's no mistaking the shape of a real telescope. "A Dobsonian reflector telescope."

"A telescope, for me? Like, my own. To keep?"

"I was going to leave it with your mother so she could give it to you on Christmas Day," he says. "But then I decided I wanted to be here, give the gift to you in person this time."

"This present is...just...amazing," I whisper.

He clears his throat. "I'll always remember my first telescope. My father saw it at a garage sale in our old neighborhood in Union City. Sometimes we'd drive a couple of counties away and set it up in a field or some suburban park. Soon I was teaching him about the constellations. I'll never forget those nights spent with my father."

I never got to meet my grandfather. He died before I was born. But I totally get what Pa's saying. This moment with him is so much better, so much more alive than postcards and pins on a map. I have real memories of him from this past month. I hope there are lots more to come.

"Lin set the viewer toward Gemini." He steps back. "Geminid meteor showers. Won't see too many, of course, with that bright three-quarter moon. But you'll still catch some."

I set my binoculars on the nearby bench and step up to the telescope. My telescope. When I glance through the eyepiece, the sky travels right to me. There is no wind or shaking hands to blur things. A still, perfect view.

We're both silent for a moment. Then I hear a faint crackle of static.

My father clears his throat. "Hope you don't mind me playing this audio. It's a feed of radio waves from the meteor shower."

Soon enough, a meteor draws a line starting in Castor and traveling across the Gemini constellation. And several seconds later my father's phone emits a high-pitched frequency. He's listening, following along with me.

"It's humbling," Pa whispers.

I lower my binoculars. "Our place in the universe, you mean?"

He takes a deep breath and then lets it out slowly. "Being here with you, after making so many mistakes." He's staring hard at me. "All I've missed out on. I do want more than postcards, Ignacio. And if you, Javi, and Christina can't come to me, well then, I guess I'm going to be making more trips to Dolton."

I'd always imagined a moment like this happening in some far off, exotic location. A desert plain in South America. Or high atop a mountain in Europe. Maybe even a remote research facility in Australia. But this moment, standing here with my father on a flat apartment roof in Dolton, New Jersey? It's the most perfect place to be in the entire universe.

# Acknowledgments

Gratitude to Northampton House Press, especially Lenore Hart and David Poyer. This book exists because of their joint expertise and steadfast guidance.

Much of the inspiration for the fictional Lenape Environmental Center came from the Meadowlands Environment Center, the Richard W. DeKorte Park Trail, the William D. McDowell Observatory, and the Rifle Camp Park Observatory. I'm grateful for the resources at these facilities, particularly Dr. John Sloan's "Let's Talk Astronomy" lecture series.

Thank you to Timothy Stefanoski of United Technologies Aerospace Systems, who provided input about astronomical equipment and hardware, and to Dr. Jennifer Walz for insight about accessibility needs in the field of scientific research, and for showing me what courage and resilience looks like in the face of extraordinary circumstances.

Many thanks to those who offered invaluable feedback on drafts of this work including Marcia Del Rios, Melissa Del Rios, Eva Del Rios-Lee, Liza Frenettc, Sandra Galfas, Yadier Johnson, Corinne O'Flynn, Gloria Pérez, Kristi Roberts, and Luz Graham Urquilla. Thank you to ShawnYaney for the outstanding cover design, and to Dr. Bonnie Culver and the entire Wilkes University Creative Writing Graduate Program for continued support.

Thanks, David Ramos, for the heat-activated constellation mug that was on my desk for much of the writing of this book, and to Heri Ramos and Gloria Pérez for sharing your love of stories and for your ongoing encouragement.

I save the biggest thank you for my amazing husband, Michael, my first reader, my rock.

# About the Author

Dania Ramos is the author of the *Seventh Grade Sleuths* series (Overdue Books/Northampton House Press). The first volume, *Who's Ju?,* was nominated for a Sakura Medal, the ILBA Mariposa Award, and won the 2015 International Latino Book Award for Best YA eBook. As a teaching artist, Dania helps children of all backgrounds share their stories through creative writing and theatre. She lives in New Jersey with her husband. Find out more at: www.daniaramos.com.

## Northampton House Press
## and Overdue Books

Established in 2011, Northampton House publishes carefully selected fiction – historical, romance, thrillers, fantasy – and lifestyle and literary nonfiction, memoir, and poetry. Our logo represents the Greek muse Polyhymnia. Overdue Books is our middle grade/young adult imprint. Check out our list at www.northampton-house.com, and Like us on Facebook – "Northampton House Press" – for more great reading!

CPSIA information can be obtained
at www.ICGtesting.com
Printed in the USA
LVHW110116221222
735707LV00004B/599